*Carol,
To the
most
wonderf...
person ...*

*For
thanks for
reading all
my shitty
1st drafts -*

FLIPKA

J.T. TWISSEL

Booktrope Editions
Seattle WA 2013

Cover Design by Melody Paris
and Kaira Paris-McDade

Edited by Cynthia White

This is a work of fiction. Names, characters, places, brands, media, and incidents are either the product of the author's imagination or are used fictitiously. Any resemblance to similarly named places or to persons living or deceased is unintentional.

PRINT ISBN 978-1-62015-155-6
EPUB ISBN 978-1-62015-251-5

For further information regarding permissions, please contact info@booktrope.com.

Library of Congress Control Number: 2013945505

ACKNOWLEDGMENTS

Many thanks to my early readers without whose encouragement I probably would not have had the courage to take a risk: Jane McKee, Carol Teltschick, Kathy Ayotte, Joel Wissmar, Bridget Gould and Cinda MacKinnon. In addition I owe a huge debt of gratitude to Judith O'Dell who tirelessly helped me get the book into shape for submission. Thanks also to the wonderful folks at Booktrope: Katherine Sears, Jesse James Freeman, Cathy Shaw, Andy, Victoria, Emily and - oh, the whole lot of you fabulous tropers! I'm such a lucky sod! I get to work with an innovative and supportive publishing company and their many delightful authors, designers and book managers who have perked up my solitary writer existence. May it live long and prosper!

I am forever grateful to have had an editor, Cynthia White, who helped me tone my voice without silencing it and a very talented pair of artists, Melody Paris and Kaira Paris-McDade who conceived a stunning design and brought it to life brilliantly. Thank you, thank you, thank you. Thank you, Julie Serra, for having enough faith in the project to sign on as book manager.

Last but not least, my apologies to the great state of Nevada.

Dedicated to JoEllen

CHAPTER 1

HE HELD A YELLOWED PHONE in one hand and a lit cigarette posed about four inches from his mouth in the other. "Yup, that's right," he coughed, pent up cigarette smoke escaping through every orifice north of his neck. "You got it. Ok, well then. Ok. If that's all you want, I got a customer, capeesh?" He slammed the receiver down. "Damn government."

His was as strange a place as I'd ever walked into in rural Nevada, and that's saying a bunch. There were only a few rows of wooden shelves, half full of packaged, canned, and bottled food — nothing fresh. In the corner several cats, frozen in various states of ire by a taxidermist, posed under a dead Christmas tree hung upside down from the rafters. The cats were clearly marked "not for sale" lest any of the many travelers drawn to his place way out in the middle of nowhere had a hankering for a stuffed cat. Luckily there was at least one refrigerated unit behind the cash register. It had been a long ride up from Vegas and I knew that where I was going the food would be institutional, unseasoned, and probably powdered—the only drinks apple juice and weak coffee sweetened with saccharin. I needed a junk food infusion to keep me going for what I hoped would only be a few days of culinary hell.

"I'm sorry, Ma'am," he coughed. "What'll it be?"

"I'll take a cold Pepsi and these Cheetos." I informed him, plopping a large bag of Cheetos on the Formica counter.

He gave me a once-over and pulled a can of Diet Pepsi from the refrigerated unit.

"I want the regular Pepsi! I might need to lose a few pounds but that diet stuff's full of chemicals!"

He looked at me as if to say your funeral, lady, and grabbed a regular Pepsi, "You come in that Nova?" he asked.

I squelched the urge to point out that mine was the only car in front of his store. "Yup. Say, where am I?"

"Pile of junk those Novas."

"It's a rental. I didn't have much of a choice."

"Wouldn't catch me in one of them piles of junk."

"Oh yeah. Well I wasn't thinking of offering you a ride, so don't worry. Now, could you kindly tell me where am I?"

"This here'd be the turn off to Steptoe," he replied. "Steptoe, Nevada, Planet Earth. You know we get a lot of Martians out here. You wouldn't be one of them, would you?"

I chuckled, mostly out of politeness. It was an old and very tired joke in that part of the world. "I'm looking for the turnoff to Fort Palmer. It's supposed to be around here somewhere. You wouldn't happen to . . ."

"Visiting somebody?"

"Yeah, you could say that."

"First road past the cattle guard. You can't miss it. There's a sign."

The phone rang again.

"Got kids?" he asked, as the phone rang unanswered.

"Nope," I replied, "I'm a . . ." Ring, ring, ring. The ringing was like fingernails against blackboard. "Hey, aren't you going to answer that phone?"

He picked up the phone and set it down speaker side up on the counter to squawk at us.

"Nope, I ain't. That'll be two-fifty, Ma'am," he replied, looking me in the eye as if to say mind your damn business. His eyes were so clouded over that the doctor in me wanted to tell him he could get help for cataracts, but I was sure that would be none of my damn business too. So I just handed him exact change and left.

Luckily for me, the sun was in no mood to set that night, hanging creamy and comforting just above the western horizon. Lord knows I needed that old sun for as long as it could afford to stick around, or at least until I found the turnoff to Fort Palmer. You can get lost real easy in the desert if you don't know where you're going—run out of gas and never be heard from again. Especially in the dark. Some people love the desert at night—the smell of mesquite, the howling of jackals under the moon. Well, they can have it.

The Pepsi picked me right up but the Cheetos, well, let's just say it's not a good idea to eat those things while driving. The chemical cheese adheres like crazy glue to the steering wheel and licking your fingers does no good; it only spreads the evidence of a Cheeto overdose to your face. Once again I pondered making a U-turn and heading home, as I had every five minutes for the past 150 miles. I'd been out of the game for a long time, but it didn't matter. I knew what to expect and I also knew damn well that going in with a crappy attitude and bright orange tongue wasn't going to win me any brownie points. What I needed was a slap across the face. Make that two slaps across the face. You're making a mountain out of a molehill, Butters. One day, maybe two is all you need and then you'll be home. No more whining and complaining. Just get on with it.

Suddenly the Nova rattled over a primitive cattle grate, dislodging the frothy Pepsi from the front seat.

"Damn!" I scowled, pulling over to the side of the road. Cattle grate. Now where was the sign I couldn't miss? The highway ahead was straighter than a ruler and, with very few kinks, would stay that way for another two hundred miles north to the Idaho border. There was no sign I couldn't miss. There was nothing. On the eastern horizon, the far-off mountains played possum in the setting sun. It had to be out there. Fort Palmer. The place where they sent the bad girls. Now where was the road?

Slowly I continued down the highway. Another five miles or so but still no sign. Had I missed it? Had the old man led me astray? Possibly. Ahead the black tar road undulated. At first I thought it was my imagination, and then I heard the first sickening crunch, followed rapidly by a second, a third, and a fourth. Soon it felt like I was driving on bubble wrap. Pop, pop, crunch. I turned on the headlights and there they were, hopping merrily across the road—an army of hard-shelled locusts. The darn things were easily the size of lab rats and there were millions of them, completely oblivious to the monster making locust jelly out of them. Now, I'm not a particularly squeamish person but driving over those creatures and hearing them crack open, knowing that their innards would create deadly slime patches on the road, added an extra ick factor to a journey that didn't need any extra ick. I beeped the horn and flashed the lights to no avail. They had no sense of fear and flooded both lanes of the highway. I had no choice but to drive over them, rationalizing with each nauseating crunch that their passing had been swift and praying I would be the only north/south traveler that night, that no teenager on a joy ride or young family on vacation hit the patch of slimy locust guts I had created.

Finally I saw a sign. It was nailed haphazardly to a fence post and read "Big Gulch Road." Now, the fact that it didn't say anything about Fort Palmer (a state facility) should have been a giant red flag, but it was the only road around, folks. And it was getting dark. So, as instructed, I turned and soon found myself on a sagebrush-filled, suspension-busting, one-lane automobile tenderizer.

Lord, I thought, as the bottom of the Nova scraped over a rock, this can't be the right road, but stubbornly I struggled down the ever-narrowing gravel pit for about a half mile until a flash of light in my rearview mirror caught my attention. It was a pickup at least twice the size of the Nova, with a rack of blinding floodlights on its roof, barreling down on me.

First thought: Desert rats hopped up on mescaline.

Second: Drunken ranch hands on their way back from a night on the town.

And there I sat. A woman all alone, soon to be dragged from the car and toyed with as if she was a mouse who'd wandered into a cat jamboree. It wouldn't matter to them if I was, say, slightly overweight or old enough to be their mother. To a man who's been in the desert too long, anything without a penis is a hot babe.

I pulled over as far as I could, hoping I would be lucky and they would whiz on past but instead they slammed on the brakes in front of me, pummeling the thin skin of the Nova with a backdraft of sand and rocks. Then, without waiting for the dust to settle, the occupants emerged: two young men in cowboy hats and aviator sunglasses. Frantically I locked the doors and reached for the bear spray I always keep in my purse.

"Howdy, Ma'am." The taller of the two said.

"Howdy, Gents," I shouted through the glass, my right hand still blindly groping through used Kleenex, loose change and breath mints for the damned bear spray.

"Ma'am, you don't want to be driving down this road."

"Why not?" I asked.

"'Cause about two miles down it washes out."

"Washes out? Then how do you get to Enev?"

"Enev?"

"I think she means that girls' prison over at Fort Palmer." The other cowboy mumbled.

"Well it's not actually a prison . . ."

"This isn't the road to Fort Palmer, Ma'am. The road you want is a couple of miles down the highway. If you want to follow us, we'll take you to it."

If they knew the road was washed out, why the heck were they on it, I thought, but miraculously, I kept my big mouth shut. "Mighty nice of you, boys. Tally ho, then!"

The cowboys managed a quick U-turn, churning through the sagebrush and bouncing off rocks. But I didn't have it so easy. My first attempt to turn that pile of crap around landed me in the soft sand on the side of the road. The second resulted in a backward lunge into a boulder. Finally the cowboys climbed down from their behemoth and came to my aid, one pushing from behind the Nova and the other in front shouting out orders.

"That was like coaxing a water buffalo out of quicksand," one of them complained, when finally I was headed in the right direction. "Here's your hubcap."

"Ha, ha! Very funny," I chuckled. "It's not my car. It's a rental."

"I hope you got insurance."

"My boss rented it. I'll let him worry about the damages." It was the least Lord God Hyman could do for disrupting my world.

About a mile down the highway an arm sprouted from the pickup, pointing to a sign by the side of the road. It clearly read "FORT PALMER" and then in smaller print beside the seal of the State of Nevada, "State Facility." They leaned on their horn until I flipped on my turn signal.

"Yeah, yeah," I said, "I see it already. I'm not completely daft!"

They stopped and watched as I turned off the highway before disappearing in the opposite direction. Washed out road, my ass, I thought as they drove away. They were protecting something at the end of Big Gulch road, something they didn't want anyone to get near. They weren't real cowboys, that was for sure. Their truck was too damned new. And where was the requisite gun rack? Or the bumper stickers touting the destruction of the Guv'mint, promoting gun rights, or touting the superiority of beer to women? Missing. No, whatever they were, they weren't cowhands. Could be military. Yeah, military fit the bill. There were all kinds of military outposts in the deserts of Nevada, places no one in their right mind wants to stumble upon. Maybe, for once in my life, I'd been lucky. Well, hot damn.

The road to Fort Palmer stretched out long and straight like a landing strip. By now it was dark and the desert sky full of thousands upon thousands of stars, some covered by pinkish clouds, thin as bridal veils. I was sure if I looked closely, I'd see a couple of UFOs. Maybe they'd even beam me up for a ride through the cosmos. (Of course, with my crappy luck, I'd get beamed aboard a gynecological research vessel!)

Lord God Hyman had implied that Fort Palmer was only about 15 minutes from the highway, so I expected to see something in the distance, the vaguest sign of life, but no. It was like driving into a dark hole. What a godforsaken place to stick these poor girls, I thought. Way out in the middle of the desert—at least one hundred miles from a McDonalds, Dairy Queen or any other necessity of teenage hell. I hate the way the system labels kids and then shuts them away. "Disturbed teen" is an oxymoron. They're all disturbed, that's the nature of being a teen.

The radio, which had been dead for hours, suddenly cackled to life, spewing forth a witch's brew of C&W, fire and brimstone, and talk-show loonies all speaking in tongues at me. I tried futzing with the dials but it was no good, every channel was such a whirling dervish of sinister voices that I killed the damn thing and put my foot all the way down on the accelerator. Whatever treadmill from hell I was on, I wanted off as soon as possible. Seventy, eighty miles an hour felt like nothing and took me nowhere. The road was still straight, the scenery exactly the same. I half expected Doctor Baby to appear on the hood—a six-feet-four, three-hundred-pound clown in diapers and carrying a baby bottle—to announce with painted-on grin that it was all a big joke; that instead of going forward, I was traveling backwards in time, slowly unfolding from staid middle age to gaa-gaa, poo-poo infancy. I pushed the car to its limits and did not stop until finally lights appeared on the horizon.

The Eastern Nevada Girls Training Facility (Enev) at Fort Palmer resembled a minimum-security prison and not a training facility, a cluster of dark barracks built into the side of a mountain and surrounded by chain-link fences topped with barbed wire. Oh Lord, I thought, is barbed wire really necessary? Where would the girls go if they escaped? They'd have to hike twenty miles across a snake-filled desert to reach the nearest highway where they could end up sitting all day waiting for a single car to even pass them by.

I drove up to the front gate and waited as the guard slowly lumbered out from his watch-shed.

"Howdy," I said.

His eyes were obscured by a low-hanging cap. All I could really see was his square jaw and no-nonsense mouth. He grunted.

"This Enev?"

He nodded.

"I'm Fiona Butters, Dr. Butters. From Vegas. I think someone is probably expecting me?"

Without speaking, he walked back to the shed, and picked up the phone. A few minutes later, the gate opened.

"Thanks," I yelled. "But where am I supposed to go?"

He pointed towards the first barracks on the right and watched as I pulled the Nova into the nearly empty parking lot. The place was so quiet, it felt like a ghost town. I took one last sip of Pepsi and climbed the metal staircase. There was no going back now.

CHAPTER 2

I AWOKE TO A BUZZER the next morning, stiffer than a mule and feeling about as cantankerous. Dinner had been Cheetos, a Pepsi and a Pepto-Bismol I'd fortunately shoved into my purse before leaving Vegas. I was hungry with a capital H.

Sunlight streamed through metal mini blinds above me but did not improve the ambiance of the room I was in; four institution-grey walls were covered with meaningless affirmation posters—"I love myself because I'm worthy"—the sort of propaganda that will drive any bright kid with an unrelenting self-loathing right over the edge. I had to fight the urge to yank the darn things off the wall and rip them to shreds, but I'd already ticked off Winnie Peterson, the Chief Administrator, Head Mistress, Warden (or whatever the heck she was called) by arriving at the very hour of her bedtime. That woman's skinny body contained not one light-hearted bone. Not one! I guessed her to be in her early fifties, a former smoker who now chewed Nicotine gum and was probably (from the style of her dress) a Mormon. That part of the state was awash with tribes of them. Of course, I'd further ingratiated myself to her by joking that 9 pm was breakfast time for me and that the ungodly hour she expected me to wake up the next morning was my bedtime. Coldly she begged me to desist from further attempts at conversation until the next morning and left me in a small room in Barracks Six with a stern admonition to "lock the door." Which I did.

In the next room I heard young girls chattering the way young girls do—in singsong short phrases, punctuated by breathless exclamations; everything was so in the moment for them, so laced with deep import and eternal consequences, that I had to snicker to myself. From the little Ms. Peterson had told me, there were just seven girls in Barracks Six, ranging in age from fifteen to seventeen. They were all from so-called good families. Their offenses against society (the things that got them there) ranged from pot-smoking and assault (generally on a parent or parental figure) to breaking and entering. One of the girls had forced open a neighbor's sliding glass patio door to steal a large bag of M&Ms that she then ate. The neighbor pressed charges and some judge, obviously a man, threw the book at her.

I threw on my sweats and wandered across the hall to the communal bathroom. Five girls stood at a row of washbasins, applying what makeup they had—sample-sized tubes of lipstick and eye shadow that were probably donated by some philanthropic women's group. The room reeked of sweet, fruity perfume. I tried not to gag.

"Hey girls!" I chortled. "Top of the morning to you! I'm Fi Butters, your new resident counselor. I got in late last night, unfortunately after light's out and dinner."

"Dinner stank." One of the girls offered as she took time from applying Cleopatra-style eyeliner to assess my reflection in the mirror. "You don't look like a counselor."

"I'm afraid to ask what I do look like. What's your name?" I asked Cleopatra.

"Thursday."

"Nice name—is that the day you were born on?"

"No. I was born on Wednesday, if my whore mother can be believed."

"Ok. How about you?" I asked the younger-looking waif close by her side. "What's your name?"

"Friday," she replied with a nervous giggle.

Spotting a trend (which would be impossible to miss unless you were brain dead), I turned to an unusually pretty blonde standing apart from the group, "I suppose your name is Tuesday?"

Cleopatra stepped in front of her, "No," she informed me. "Tuesday isn't here—she's getting dressed. That's Monday."

The pretty blonde rolled her eyes.

"Ok, ok," I laughed, drawing a one in the air, "The Days of the Week 1, Butters 0." The joke fell flatter than a pancake. I was about to make another attempt at communication when a bell announced the call to breakfast and off they trotted like stampeding colts.

"My name is Merry, not 'Monday'," the blonde beauty informed me as she sauntered away a bit more gracefully than the others, "and I don't play Nancy Jean's stupid games."

Aha, "Thursday" was Nancy Jean and "Monday" was Merry. No telling who Friday really was. This is going to be a lot of fun, I thought to myself, a lot of fun.

After completing my very brief ablutions, I decided to take a look around the now-empty barracks. In the large room next to my hole-in-the-wall were two rows of twin-size beds opposite each other, headboards pushed against the walls. Each was next to a small unadorned dresser, big enough for socks, underwear, and jammies but not much else. The floor was cold linoleum, bleached from a sandy color through the obvious over application of Lysol. Gag. The walls contained many nicks and greasy splotches as if little effort was put into correcting the damage done by the tenants. There was just one window, along the southern end of the room, and it was barred. The only door led to the hall between my room and the bathroom. Down the hall in the other direction was a sitting room with four well-used sofas set around a wood coffee table, a bookshelf filled with well-used paperbacks and writing supplies, and the front door.

I dressed quickly and then waited in the front room for the promised escort to breakfast, a three-ringed binder titled Eastern Nevada Girls Reformatory, Procedures and Policies (my required reading) on my lap. According to this document, girls in minimum security were expected to wake up at 6:00 am and be at the Mess by 6:30 to set up for breakfast. Girls on reprimand stayed after breakfast to wash dishes. Everyone else had one half hour for exercise in the quad (good weather) or in the gym (bad weather). The rest of the morning was spent in vocational training. The afternoons were reserved for group counseling or meeting with counselors to review their individualized independent study programs. Fridays were reserved for cleanup and laundry. Weekends were for visits from family but in most cases probably served as a painful reminder of how far they were from home: five hours from the major population centers of Reno and Vegas and an hour from the nearest hotel or restaurant. That would be enough to discourage visits from even the most adoring of parents.

There were two types of non-prisoners at Enev: resident counselors, who lived in the dormitories with the girls and supervised their activities, and field counselors, who drove out from wherever they lived a couple of times a week to provide vocational training, counseling, and help with independent study programs. Resident counselors served as a combination prison guard and mother hen and were expected to live at the facility 24/7. The incentive for this enormous sacrifice was a week of vacation every month and, after three years of service, a five-month sabbatical with full pay. I was expected to impersonate a resident counselor, to pass myself off as a replacement for the one who disappeared. According to Hyman, this brilliant strategy would enable me to find out what was really going on in Barracks Six. But there was one small problem. It had taken the Days of the Week exactly two seconds to see right through me. I'm not exactly sure what they saw but for darned sure, it wasn't a mother hen/prison guard.

I was almost finished skimming through all the various security procedures when Miss Peterson arrived to collect me for breakfast. In her arms she carried a pile of green folders.

"Thank God, you're here," I told her, "I was down to my last breath mint! I'm so hungry I was about to raid the girl's dressers for contraband!"

"I was collecting the girls' files for you, Dr. Butters. Of course, they're all highly confidential, so you'll have to review them at Palmer House after breakfast." She explained as we walked across a quad of tightly mowed crabgrass toward a three-story Victorian set on the hill above the barracks. "Since you're not certified in this state, I shouldn't even be letting you touch them. I told Mr. Hyman that but he's so . . ."

"Charmingly persuasive?" I interrupted, with a chuckle.

"Just don't say anything to the other counselors."

Lord, the woman was paranoid. "Listen, I'm only here because Doug Hyman's ex-wife has a few loose screws. That's all. You know, I can't remember who got slaughtered here," I laughed. "Was it the Cavalry or the Indians?"

"No one got slaughtered here, Dr. Butters."

"Oh yeah? Wasn't Fort Palmer the site of a massacre?"

"Let me tell you something Dr. Butters—"

"Fi, please."

"The Indian wars in this part of the state were little more than dust-ups between the ranchers and loosely knit tribes of desert squatters: raggedy bands of drifters, living off lizards and snakes—really, hardly a match for the cavalry."

"So there was no massacre? How disappointing. How about that graveyard up on the hill? Cowboys and Indians?"

"No. Miners. There was a mining settlement here once. They couldn't move the graves, of course, so they put the outer fence just on the other side of the graveyard. I don't think it was proper for them to enclose a graveyard within the walls of a girls' reformatory but that was before my time. The girls aren't allowed up there, of course."

"Of course, but I was thinking mud. It looks a little greener up there than the rest of the facility."

"Mud?" She stopped in her tracks as if I'd shot her.

"Yes—I thought the morning after the counselor's disappearance, you found mud all over the girls' room and on their shoes."

"How can that be important? So their shoes were dirty. So what?"

"I heard on the radio on the way up that the first rainstorm of the season is set to hit eastern Nevada this weekend—and it sure doesn't look like anything around here ever gets watered, so, where did they find the mud to waddle about in?"

"Are you a psychiatrist or a detective, Dr. Butters?"

"Good point," I chuckled. We were standing in the shadow of Palmer House beyond which I could see the summit of Cavalry Peak, silhouetted by the rising sun. Even after a long dry summer, there was snow on the summit.

"Don't expect a Vegas-style breakfast," she warned as we entered Palmer House. "This is a state-run facility. Grab something and then we'll have breakfast with the staff. I'm sure you'll have lots of questions for them."

"I shouldn't be exposed to other people on an empty stomach," I chuckled. "Can I just sit by myself and have a moment?"

The look on her face said no. Her "staff" watched me from the long ranch-style table centered in the middle of the room. I counted

maybe six of them. It had been years—almost a decade—since I'd
seen the look they gave me: Who the hell does she think she is with
her Ivy League degree and early and easy accomplishments?

"My staff may not have your impressive background, Doctor.
But we're all professionals."

Oh lord, I thought as I grabbed a couple of stale-looking pastries
and a small red apple and followed her to the table.

"For those of you who haven't heard about Dr. Butters," Winnie
began, after she'd briefly introduced me to the people sitting at the
table. There was a nurse who came to Enev every other week, a man
and a woman who provided vocational training and three other
resident counselors. Frankly, I didn't pay too much attention to the
introductions as I figured I wouldn't be around long enough for it to
matter. "She spent several years on the staff of UMass in the 1970s
teaching abnormal psychology. During that time she wrote several
important papers on hysteria in the adolescent female and is considered
one of the world's leading authorities on the so-called Salem complex.
Dr. Butters left psychiatry several years ago and has been working in
Vegas as a—What was it, Dr. Butters?—a set designer?"

"Actually," I said, mouth full of pastry, "I'm in charge of the
props. And it's a hoot! A real hoot! The acrobats call me 'The Queen
of Props'."

The gentleman at the end of the table smiled: "So you ran away
and joined the circus."

"Yup," I laughed, "I guess you could put it that way."

"Anyway," Winnie Peterson continued, "now she's here to
observe the behavior of the girls in Barracks Six and provide us with
a recommendation as to how to proceed. The girls have been told
that she's their new resident counselor."

"Are you here to do an exorcism on those little witches, because
that's what they need," the nurse bluntly set forth. I had to give her a
second look. She didn't look that dumb—what were they teaching in
nursing school these days?

"Hell no. I'm not even Catholic. In fact, I'm not even Christian—
at least not this week. Adolescent females are full of raging hormones,
just like their male counterparts; only for females, the by-product of
those rages can mimic what we have been conditioned to believe is

abnormal behavior—trances, visions, and even seizures. Especially girls in a restricted environment. Rarely is there a causal effect, such as supernatural interference. Don't get me wrong—I have nothing against a little supernatural interference every now and then, but 99.9 percent of these cases are simply examples of hormones run amok."

"How about the incident at the Monson Academy?" Winnie Peterson asked.

Well, she'd actually read one of my papers, I thought. But the million-dollar question was: Had she read the entire case history or the adulterated version I'd been forced to publish? I strongly doubted it was the former.

"That's a case I'm afraid I can't discuss. The litigants in the bee-zillion lawsuits that followed will be in court longer than Jarndyce v Jarndyce."

CHAPTER 3

OVER BREAKFAST I reluctantly heard the story of the former counselor of Barracks Six whose disappearance from the facility two weeks earlier, sans car, wallet or Bible, still rattled the staff. The White Pine County Sheriff's theory—that she had a secret boyfriend with whom she'd run off—left them shaking their heads in disbelief. She was apparently not that kind of girl. But, since there was no blood, no trail, just a pile of muddy shoes and uncooperative teens, the case had been closed.

"Really, folks," I began in an attempt to placate, "I gotta tell you that young women disappear all the time (especially in this neck of the woods) and often the police are right. She might have met some guy she knew mom and dad wouldn't approve of, and so, instead of disappointing them or creating a conflict, she set up a mysterious disappearance. Sometimes young women disappear because they crave the notoriety. They want to see their picture on the news or hear their loved ones plead for their return. Who knows? There are as many reasons for these disappearances as there are stars in the sky."

It wasn't that I didn't care about the missing counselor, but I was sure the staff's perceptions about events of the last couple of weeks had now been prejudiced by the arrival of someone like me. This is not an egotistical statement, but the arrival of a quote-unquote expert in abnormal psychology at a remote location manned by a few minimally trained though good-hearted professionals would color any remembrance of odd events. Imagine. Someone disappears from work one day, and suddenly the next day, the employers are ushered into a conference room to confer with Sherlock Holmes (not that I am Sherlock Holmes but it is the best example I can come up with at the moment). What do you think the employees would assume? Besides, I wasn't there to solve the mystery of the missing counselor.

After breakfast Winnie Peterson's staff retreated to offices on the second level of Palmer House to prepare for their classes. I sat at the long table, as ordered, to review the case files of the girls in Barracks Six, but there was really only one I was interested in: the file belonging to the daughter of Doug Hyman. She was, after all, the reason I was there in the first place.

Wealthy, powerful men are rarely beauties, but Hyman took the cake. His publicity shots, posted all over Vegas, led one to assume that, yes, he might need a lot of work done on his face, and yes, he wore an obnoxious toupee, but to actually see him live and unaltered was such a shock that I spent most of our first meeting wondering how he hid his tail. Of course, my expectations upon that first meeting could not have been more ludicrous. I actually thought he sent a man in an expensive-looking Perry Ellis suit down into the bowels of the casino to fetch me because he'd seen one of my Christmas window displays and said, "Wow, what an artist!" You see, aside from working backstage on the holidays, I pick up extra cash painting Santas and Easter bunnies on storefront windows. So, of course the answer to the perplexing question of why the head of several casinos on the Vegas strip would demand to see a lowly stagehand had to be that he wanted me to decorate the windows of the Bellagio with cartoons of Santa. Ridiculous, I know, but I couldn't think of any other reason.

There is nothing more surreal than a penthouse view in Vegas. Imagine floor-to-ceiling windows looking out over the pastel pink and blue spires of the castle at the Disney Excalibur and beyond, mountains ripped from tarpaper silhouetted against a sapphire sky. Really, Salvador Dali could not have imagined a more surrealistic scene than the Vegas landscape from Doug Hyman's penthouse office.

"Come over here, pul—eeze." The man himself sat with his back against the wall in the corner of the room, surrounded by a massive burl-top table, the paneling behind him covered with plaques and pictures of celebrities. There were three buffalo-skin chairs with antler-inspired wooden arms on the other side of the desk. I chose the one in the middle.

"Fiona isn't it?"

"Yup," I replied, "Mr. Hyman, isn't it?"

"Don't be cute. It doesn't become you."

"Say, how do you get around that monster desk?"

"I don't," he explained as he pushed a button on the desk and a piece of the paneling moved slightly, "I only use this office to meet with people. I'm like Heff. I like to do most of my work in the bedroom on the other side of this wall. But I don't like people to see my bed."

I wasn't going to touch that line with a ten-foot pole.

"The set manager, what's his name?" He continued. His eyes were the color of split pea soup. No wonder the Russians thought he was the Antichrist.

"Sergei," I responded.

"Yeah, Sir Gee. He kept telling me your name was Flipper, like that stupid fish show."

"It's Flipka. Flipka is a Russian term of endearment meaning a difficult broad." I joked. "Those Russian acrobats just love me."

He scowled. "Those Russians. What a pain in the ass it is to deal with them!"

I laughed. My Russian acrobats had nerves of steel, swinging upside down one-hundred feet off the ground, all the while smacking gum and making shopping lists in their heads. I had to admire them, although I wouldn't want to have to negotiate with them in any way regarding money; they'd slice you open for shorting them a dime, even a guy like Hyman.

"Anyway, I'll get right down to business, because I've got casinos to run. I know who you really are, Butters." He announced, as though he had just solved a deep, dark mystery. "You're a shrink!"

"So what?" I replied.

"So, what are you doing working on my props?"

"Midlife crisis. I suppose you started out wanting to run a casino and never thought of being anything else?" I quipped.

He grimaced for a second and then played his second card: "And not only that, I know about Monson Academy."

"Mr. Hyman, why don't you tell me what this is all about? I'm not a mind reader."

"You ever hear of Enev?"

"Enev. Oh yeah, where all the bad girls go. I was born in Battle Mountain, Mr. Hyman."

"Yes I know," he replied, "I know everything about you."

"I don't know why."

"Let me tell why I made it my business to know all about you, Butters. My daughter, the one from the third marriage," he said holding up three fingers, "is a little confused. She's got a crazy mother but she's a sweet girl, beautiful girl, just—confused. Got herself into some trouble that I couldn't get her out of. It's a long story, but anyway, she's at Enev. At first I thought—well, what the heck, it might do her some good, you know. It was better than her hanging out with all them hippies. But now I don't know."

Doug Hyman, King of Vegas, hadn't been able to save his daughter from a hellhole like Enev, where unwanted and rebellious girls were sent by their families to teach them a lesson in obedience? Something was definitely not kosher.

He continued with his story.

"My ex-wife (the crazy bitch) has been on the phone nonstop, yammering away at me day and night. Apparently the girls in with my daughter have been getting out at night and the geniuses up there can't figure out how. Now a counselor has disappeared and the girls are acting wacko. Some idiot told my wife they were possessed by the Devil."

"What do the police say?" I responded. "I mean about the disappearance of the counselor?"

"Police! Huh!" He laughed. "The White Pine County Sheriff! Don't make me laugh, Doc. Anyway, I don't care about some two-bit counselor."

"I don't know what you expect me to do. I'm not a detective or a priest, you know. I'm not even a shrink anymore. I'm the prop lady for one of your shows, and I sometimes paint Easter bunnies in store windows."

"Easter bunnies! Christ! Listen, my ex has had therapy up the wing-wang. It's sort of a hobby with her, you know what I mean? Primal screaming and something called est, you name it, she's tried it. Anyway, her current shrink, some shyster living off rich divorcées up at Tahoe, tells her that she needs to fish up some expert in witchcraft by the name of Dr. Butters."

"I'm not an expert in witchcraft."

"You think I believe in that crap? Hell no. But the Ex does. And she knows that I have these sources, and they can find anybody in the whole friggin' world, anybody. We have to—you know, to do business. So just to shut her up, I agree to find this wacky broad for her. Imagine my surprise to find you right downstairs. Friggin' small world, huh?"

"It's a small world, but there's one big problem. I'm not licensed to practice psychiatry anywhere on the west coast and that includes Nevada."

"That's not a problem."

And that's how I ended up at Enev, on a mission to report my expert opinion on whether or not the ground had opened up and swallowed the missing counselor because a group of teenaged girls had conjured forth the Devil. Fun, hey? And if I didn't come back with the right diagnosis, the ugliest man on the planet would have me deported to Siberia.

The first file I picked up contained the lovely mug shot of the girl with the Cleopatra makeup. Stage name: Thursday. Actual name: Nancy Jean. She had been convicted of assault and destruction of property. Apparently many legal slaps on the wrist had helped her socialite mother make the case to the authorities that her daughter was incorrigible. How could the apple fall so far from the tree? Take her away, Officer; lock her up. There's nothing I can do. Her psych evaluation cited self-mutilation, insomnia and possible borderline schizophrenia. My guess would be a depressed teenage girl with a narcissistic mother.

The second file belonged to Bonny B., previously a ward of the state, accused of theft multiple times, bounced from foster home to foster home until finally convinced by a boyfriend to help him rob a gas station. Above average IQ but a compulsive liar with low self-esteem. Bonny looked directly into the camera in her picture, large brown eyes innocent; makeup perfect. So much for Winnie Peterson's assertion that all the girls in Barracks Six were from good families. Unless she considered the State of Nevada a good parental figure, that is.

The third file belonged to Leticia H., a pale, fragile-looking waif who'd never learned to smile. A chronic runaway, she had been found guilty of solicitation and was on a combination of antidepressants. She was the girl introduced to me as Friday. According to the file, she had a grandfather in the area, under a restraining order issued by the Sheriff at the request of Winnie Peterson.

The fourth file belonged to Meredith Hyman, who liked to be called Merry. She'd been convicted of possession of marijuana with intent to sell. I was shocked. Who would have ever guessed that a creature like Doug Hyman could produce such a pretty daughter?

CHAPTER 4

IF THE EYES ARE THE WINDOWS to the soul, the taste buds are the autobahn to the brain. It's true, believe me. You can't possibly communicate with a group of teenage girls over dried apricots. It just can't be done. I needed chocolate and there was certainly none to be had at Enev.

"I've got to take a drive," I informed Winnie Peterson as I returned the girls' files to the office for lockdown. "I'll be back just after lunch."

She was aghast. I had just gotten there; I hadn't really met or talked to the girls, and now I was leaving? Luckily, the arrival of fresh new inmates temporarily distracted her. Hooray for the cavalry, I thought, as I watched five young ladies stumble out of a State of Nevada van, this week's catch of bad girls from all over the state. My own little darlings were busy learning to be happy homemakers, along with a dozen or so other young ladies from the other barracks, in the stainless steel kitchen of the dining barracks.

There were six other barracks, each containing from seven to twelve girls. They sat facing each other across a rectangular weed patch, where in the late 1860s, young men fresh from the Midwest and other points east had marched in formation, pumped up to fight the mighty Injun who turned out to be a squat locust eater unaware the land had been appropriated by the Great White God. After the cavalry left, the fort sat vacant, acid-washed by the wind until it resembled Stonehenge. Fort Palmer's recent history was as murky as a dirty fish tank, which meant only one thing: the current structures had been built by the Feds, probably during the early years of atomic testing, and populated by human guinea pigs.

The old man at the store near Steptoe recognized me right off and chuckled as I plopped down several bags of Hershey's kisses, Rolos, and Ding Dongs on the counter.

"What are you doing in these parts?" He asked. "I thought you were just visiting someone over at Fort Palmer."

"I confess. I'm working there."

"Enev?" he asked.

"Yup."

"What are you doing?"

"I'm a nutritionist."

He examined the bags of candy and chuckled. "That so?"

"Hey, have you ever had to deal with a group of teenage girls?"

"Damned Feds. They shouldn't a put them girls out there," he growled.

"It is a hellish place, I agree, but it's no longer a federal facility— it belongs to the state." (I don't know why I always insist on pointing out irrelevant facts. In psych terms, it's called anal retention.)

"The Lechtay live inside Cavalry Peak you know," he muttered as he rang the bags of candy and other assorted goodies. "That's what happened to that woman who disappeared. The Lechtay got her. That'll be eight fifty, ma'am."

Ok, I thought, the old guy's probably lived out in the desert a little too long. "I heard that all the Indians are in Utah now," I countered, as I handed him nine bucks. "On some reservation. Keep the change."

"The Lechtay ain't Indians."

"Then what are they? Bats?"

"If I tell you, you probably won't believe me. But they got that woman, you know. They did, but the government covered it all up."

"Well, hell. The government always covers everything up, doesn't it? Aliens might be living among us but the government will cover it up. Heck, maybe the government is run by the aliens. Or maybe—an even scarier premise—it might be run by humans just like us. Thanks for the warning. But I'm from Vegas – land of vampires and werewolves. I think I can handle a few Lechtays."

"Suit yourself but I warned you."

As I drove back toward Enev, I began to wonder how the news of the counselor's disappearance made its way across the state to the third ex-Mrs. Hyman, currently of Lake Tahoe. According to Doug Hyman, the story hadn't even warranted a bullet in the police blotter of the Ely Times. It made sense that rumors would leak to the locals (like the shopkeeper), but we were a long way from Tahoe, and in my experience, young ladies generally don't call their mothers to report that they're possessed by the devil. In the scheme of things, it was a relatively minor detail but since it was the detail that got me into this pickle in the first place, it was the detail I chose to crucify, as I cursed my way back across the valley of the slippery locust guts.

At the gates of Enev, I crossed paths with the state van. Watching it depart was Winnie Peterson, her dust-bowl face withered in the bright sunshine. Three of her girls were on the bus, she told me. Two headed for an adult detention facility; the third released, but having no home, soon to be dropped off on the streets of Vegas with a small amount of cash and list of referrals. I guess some things never go down easy, no matter how hard-hearted a face you show the world. I offered her a Twinkie and saw her lust for it as a child would a forbidden toy.

"No thanks."

"You sure?"

"Yes."

"You really, really sure?"

"Dr. Butters, two of your girls had an incident after breakfast." She bluntly informed me.

"What do you mean?"

"A fight."

"Do we know why?"

"They wouldn't say. We could have used your professional expertise to deal with the situation."

Christ Almighty. I'd been there less than twenty-four hours. "Maybe they just hate each other," I suggested.

"Well, they'll be spending the weekend in detention. Meanwhile, the other girls are waiting in the barracks—if you wouldn't mind interviewing them so that we can get on with this farce."

And so the Days of the Week were now five. The three I'd met in the bathroom (Meredith Hyman, Nancy Jean of the Cleopatra eyeliner, and poor little Leticia) and the two I hadn't met: Bonnie, the foster child, and Thanh, a Vietnamese girl for whom there was a missing rap sheet and no psych eval. They awaited my arrival with such funereal faces that I suggested a nice walk up to the graveyard behind Palmer House might cheer them up.

"The graveyard?" They echoed, almost in unison.

"Yeah—why not?"

"That's stupid. There's nothing to see up there," Nancy Jean supplied with all the haughtiness of a Siamese cat.

"Au contraire, it's a hoot to read the inscriptions on old tombstones, don't you think? Here lies old Tom; he was buried with his boots on. That kind of thing."

"That is so stupid!"

"Really, then why have you girls been sneaking up there in the middle of the night?"

That hushed her royal prickliness for a couple of seconds. "Oh, that's so stupid. How can we sneak out when we're locked in every night? We can't even go pee in the middle of the night if we have to!"

The logic cells of a girl's brain are the last to develop. And yet, the little pea pickers have this notion that they are logic personified. It never fails to amaze me how they can take one fact and use it to try to camouflage any number of obvious details in a scenario. The doors lock, therefore we were locked in.

"Then how come during the very dry month of September, you gals managed to get your shoes muddy when you were supposed to be sleeping? And, because the only place around here that looks well watered is the grove of pinyons above the graveyard, I'm betting that's where you've been heading. Although I can't for the life of me imagine why. Is there an old artesian well up there that provides a bit of moonlit entertainment?"

"Did you not hear me?" Nancy Jean threatened. "We're locked in every night!"

The higher her voice rose, the more she confirmed that my arrow was on target.

"I think the bottle of brandy I found stashed under your counselor's bed might explain a few things, don't you?" I proceeded. "She had a problem, didn't she?"

There was a group gasp, a rapid exchange of looks, and then Nancy Jean took control again: "You're guessing."

"You're absolutely right. I'm guessing. But I'm pretty good, aren't I?"

"You are so weird."

"I'm weird? According to what I've heard about you gals, you've been incanting all kinds of bad voodoo against your innocent counselors and other inmates, summoning demons from the underworld and . . ."

"That's not true!" Meredith interrupted, "that's not what we're doing at all!"

"Shut up!" Nancy Jean hissed. "Everybody just shut up."

And that's exactly what they did.

CHAPTER 5

IN THE EVENING I was summoned to the superintendent's office like a wayward girl in trouble with the principal.

"How did my session with the girls go?" I replied to her question of the same content. "Pretty darned good. In fact I managed to get all the little darlings to clam up tighter than Fort Knox. Now they won't even look at me."

It was not the response that Winnie Peterson expected. The sun was setting on my first day and I had not produced the requested miracle.

"And you think it's a good thing that they're not talking to you? I thought the point of therapy was to get a person to open up, not clam up."

I fingered an extra pack of Rolos stashed in my coat pocket, thinking how good one would taste, especially as the hard wooden chair in her office offered scant comfort. Milk chocolate and caramel, now slightly melted by my warm anxious fingers. Yum.

"I do think the session went extremely well," I replied.

"I don't understand."

"Means I've stumbled onto at least one of their little secrets, maybe two. No, that's not a maybe but a positively. Positively two. Do you play poker, Miss Peterson?"

She looked perplexed. I decided I didn't care if I was being rude. I ripped into the Rolos and thrust one of those little darlings into my mouth as she watched. The warm chocolate coated my fingertips, but not for long. "Look at it this way," I continued, licking my fingers. "They've closed ranks because they think I know more than I do and if they clam up, I won't find out the rest. Ha! That's the mind of the teenage girl for you."

Winnie Peterson wanted a cigarette badly. It was rude and nasty and childish of me to indulge in my weakness and watch her suffer.

"Care for a Rolo?" I asked. "Slightly better for you than a cigarette."

"No."

"They're not all melted. I think I can find . . ."

"No, thank you."

We sat in the quiet for a few minutes. Outside the wind was picking up, the first storm of the season trucking rapidly off the salt flat, blowing sand and tumbleweeds across the parking lot. The staff counselors had all departed for the weekend, leaving only a skeleton crew to tackle the dreary weekend. Two movies were planned: one on Saturday and the other on Sunday. Both PG.

"Where are you from, Winnie?" I asked, "I have a bet going with myself that you're a transplant to these parts."

"I'm waiting for you to tell me what their secret is, Dr. Butters. I've got a facility to shut down as you know and five new girls to check on."

"Are you going to get a chance to drive home and see the family this weekend?" I asked, noting the photograph of Winnie standing over a man in a wheelchair that sat behind her on a credenza.

"Please Dr. Butters. Their secret."

"Oh," I mumbled, "that's a shame. Well, maybe next weekend, hey? All work and no play, you know."

"Dr. Butters!"

"Well, it was a guess really, which they confirmed with adamant denial and later complete silence."

"What do you mean?"

"Did the police find any empty brandy bottles when they searched the missing counselor's room or her car?"

"Are you suggesting she had a drinking problem, because I'll have to stop you right there; she was a good Mormon."

"What else can you tell me about her?"

"Not much. She'd only been with us a couple of years—in February she would have qualified for her sabbatical, so it just doesn't make much sense that she'd disappear." Winnie looked at me for some explanation, but I just shrugged. People disappear all the time from lives others envy.

She continued. "Well, let's see. What else do I know about her? She's thirty-five. Never married. Like many of our resident counselors, she'd wanted to be in law enforcement but didn't quite make the mark for some reason or other. It's not easy recruiting counselors for Enev. They generally hang around until their first sabbatical, and then they're gone."

Aha, I thought, alcohol had found a happy breeding ground in the garden of the defeated, those self-sentenced to three years of teenage contemptuousness for their failures. She must have known her secret would soon be out. But how? The lovelies would have never threatened her. They had a good thing going.

"If you think about it," I continued, "that's the only thing that makes sense. The mother hen got wasted and the chicks flew the coop. Did the police search her car? I'll bet they found a pile of empties hidden in her trunk."

Winnie Peterson was speechless. I decided to backtrack a little.

"You know I'm only just guessing about the counselor. But since I've shut up a group of teenage girls who know everything, I think I came close to hitting the nail on the hammer—or hitting the nail with the hammer—however, the damned phrase goes."

"What do I say to Mr. Hyman if he calls?"

"He's not going to call on a Friday night. But if he does, tell him it is my professional opinion that his daughter is not possessed, and I'll be home tomorrow if he wants to drag me up to his office/bedroom and throw me to the lions. You don't need to tell him about the brandy or any of my other half-cocked theories about the missing counselor. That'll just be between the two of us."

Chapter 6

WHEN THE RAIN HIT, I was in the middle of a nightmare. My very first one, and let me tell you, it was a whopper, transforming old "I never dream" Butters into a quivering, sweat-saturated, paranoid schizophrenic, certain the Devil lurked in her unconsciousness, panting with desire for her to sleep so that he could rip her soul from her body in the most grotesque and painful way possible. The monster under the bed, the ogre in the closet—the Nazguls from the land of Sauron—all had taken up residence in my mind.

And it was Karma; well-deserved payback. You see, for years I'd counseled people with sleep disorders, rambling off various theories on unresolved traumatic stress, even though I had not the vaguest clue of the depth of terror my patients felt. Not the foggiest, because I never dreamt, let alone nightmared. My peers will tell you it's impossible not to dream. We all dream. We might not all remember our dreams, but we all dream. In graduate school my insistence that I was the lone exception to this rule earned me instant membership in the "Dream Clinic of the Month" club. I was always the first enlisted to test a new dream theorem, summoned to a clinic, strapped into the proper recording devices, put to sleep, woken up at various times during the night by caffeine-laden grad students, and questioned. Always with the same response: I remembered nothing. Several theories were proposed as to my abnormal psyche, one for each branch of psychotherapy. My favorite was that I was a psychopath with no conscience. Apparently demons never dream. I finally ended my participation in such nonsense when the cognitive neurologists wanted to put electrical probes in my brain. Now really, folks, who would trust a graduate student to insert something into their brain?

However it didn't seem fair that I'd gotten my comeuppance about as far from an ivy-school dream lab as can be, quivering like a child beneath an army blanket, as thunder rumbled over the desert. I fumbled for the lamp on the nightstand. It crashed to the floor. It was then that I heard the chanting:

Father come to us
Mother come to us
Brother come to us
Bring us back our bows

At first I thought I was still unconscious, that the nightmare still held tight to my poor brain. Pick an object to concentrate on, I told myself, turn away and then look back at it. Has it changed? If yes, dream. If no, awake. It was a trick I learned at one of my many sleep labs, a trick I'd never had to use until now. If you can't decide whether you're dreaming or awake, focus on an object, turn away and then glance back at the object. If the object has changed in any way, you're still in the dream. If it is exactly the same, chances are you're awake. The theory being that dreams are made up of image imprints that flash through our dream cycles, which is why you can be dreaming about your father when suddenly his face transforms into that of your husband. This does not mean that you have an oedipal attraction to your father, as the Freudians might deduce. It just means the guy running the slide project in your brain has a warped sense of humor.

I decided to focus on the painting of Jesus hung on the wall opposite my bed, because highlighted by flashes of lightning, he reminded me of Elvis. One of those Elvis-on-black-velvet paintings that you see sold on the streets. Lord almighty, I feel my temperature rising. I stared at it a few moments, looked away quickly and then back. OK, he was holding the same pose. One hand upraised popelike. That was a good sign. I was awake, as were the little lovelies now chanting their pea-picking hearts out in the next room. I quickly threw on my bathrobe and slippers, and then, forgetting Winnie Peterson's prime directive—"before you do anything in a suspicious situation, ring the guard"—unlocked the door.

The next thing I remember was waking up back in bed, the light streaming through the aluminum blinds, my head pounding. Jesus, crooked on the wall, and a faint whiff of something sweetly foul in the air.

Whatever they'd done all night, the little shits were now sleeping peacefully in their beds. But not for long.

"They broke out of the corral again last night," I informed Winnie Peterson"In the middle of the rainstorm, so you can imagine the scene in their room. Right now, I've got the little lovelies on their hands and knees scrubbing the whole place down. I told them no breakfast until it was spotless."

She'd looked up from her paperwork with scorn. "They snuck out?"

"Yup."

"How do you explain their escape this time, Dr. Butters – were you drinking?"

"No mystery there. I let them out. The question is, what the heck are they doing?"

"You let them out?"

"Not on purpose. I heard them chanting and, without thinking, unlocked the door to their room. After that I don't know what happened; I woke up on top of my bed, frozen as a cherry popsicle with a headache the size of New Hampshire."

At this point, things got really squirrelly. Obviously, she snorted, I had been wrong. This was not simply the matter of a group of girls taking advantage of a drunken counselor. "If only I hadn't been so hesitant," she grumbled.

"To call a priest?" I joked.

"Don't be silly. That would be like reporting flying saucers over Enev."

"Do you?"

"That's not the point. I should have put them all in detention where they belong the minute this first began."

"Except for Meredith Hyman, right? By the way, where did her mother get the notion that evil spirits had taken over Enev?"

"I don't know. Certainly not from anyone at the school."

"Are you sure? Maybe the missing counselor got in touch with her."

"I thought you were leaving, Dr. Butters."

"'Cause, you know, whatever they're up to, they're all in it together. I read them the riot act and not one peep. Except Nancy Jean, who claimed that I'd come in to check on them, tripped, and knocked myself out. And then the little darlings put me back into bed out of the caring compassion of their souls. Ha! Don't you love that one? I'm sure they didn't honestly expect me to fall for it, but what the heck, they gave it a shot. That's teens for you. Always taking the long shot."

But Winnie wasn't listening to a word I said. In her book I was already gone. She picked up the walkie-talkie on her desk and ordered whoever was on the other side to retrieve Nancy Jean from Barracks Six and lock her in detention. According to her, Nancy Jean was the obvious mastermind; the girl who had whacked me over the head and was leading the other girls down the path to destruction. I listened as she went on and on, knowing that I was not hit over the head, but tranquilized. I also knew Nancy Jean might be the loudmouth, but she was not the leader.

I thought of telling her what I'd found after waking the sleeping beauties with an off-key rendition of "Wake Up Little Susie", and sending them (accompanied by the guard) to the mess hall for extra mops and pails. What I'd found shoved between the mattresses of Meredith Hyman's bed as I poked through their things. But I didn't. I slipped into my professional voice and told her sternly:

"Separating the girls is not going to solve the problem. It will only spread the contagion to the other barracks. Give me another night with them. I have a fairly good idea what possesses the Days of the Week."

"What?"

"I'd rather not say right now. Just give me another day."

Of course she wasn't in favor of this plan. She demanded to know what my idea was, but I knew what her response would be, and so I kept my mouth shut. "If I'm right, I'll tell you tomorrow morning," I promised. Finally she agreed, but she assured me, if I did not produce a story worthy of Scheherazade, it would be curtains for Fi Butters.

CHAPTER 7

THE HANDWRITING WAS ELEGANT, polished, and near perfect, done probably with a quill and precious black ink in a leather-bound diary, grown ochre with age. It purported to be the journal of a young cavalryman, a Major Sebastian Olivore, 11ᵗʰ Cavalry, B Troop; the paper was yellowed and brittle, the content and style fitting for a reasonably well-educated gent of the nineteenth century. There were only three cogent entries, the remaining pages filled with hieroglyphic drawings and random words. Pages appeared to be missing, but the journal was so old, it was hard to tell. Still, it was easy to understand how young Sebastian's plight had captivated my little lovelies:

The Journal of Major Sebastian Olivore, 11ᵗʰ Cavalry, B Troop
April 26, 1865. I am in your hands, oh Lord, where the land is hard and water scarce. I try not to dwell on the beauty I left behind, the tall spring grasses and abundant bounties of home, to embark upon this mission to protect the Overland Stagecoach from Indian savages. I struggle to embrace this dry desert as part of thy mysterious wonder; however, Lord, it is hard to recognize thy goodness in such a cruel setting, a sign without doubt of the weakness of my faith. Thank you for the blessing of this journal, delivered to me this morn by none other than the crew of the stagecoach, who, with their clientele, are at present enjoying a much-needed repast. What brave men are the men of the stagecoach, struggling on their own across the wide and endless expanse of dried lakebeds and venomous insects where many souls have perished. I must suspend my ruminations to pen a letter to my father, the giver of this journal. It distresses me much to know that father believes our endeavors here in the wilderness are noble, but I will leave him to his comforts. SO

May 6, 1865. Oh Lord, in this land where water is squeezed from rock, flowers of a sort have begun to bloom on the tips of various cacti – a curious plant which we have not in North Carolina. The Spanish claim with much certainty that some of these plants provide milk to those lost in the desert. First you must get beyond unimaginable spines. 'T is just another of the unfathomable mysteries and oddities of the lands west of the Rocky Mountains.

The Spanish are on hand to direct construction of barracks for the volunteer militia who serve gallantly with us. At present our fort consists merely of two buildings of rock construction, used also as a way house for the stagecoach, a flotilla of canvas tents, and a corral for the horses. Our men are aided in their hard labor by a group of dark-skinned men traveling with the Spanish whom the troops first misidentified as slaves. This led to a few incidents successfully mediated by Colonel Palmer. My lantern is low on oil this eve. I must surrender to the dark. The music of the Spanish guitars has ceased and so the campfire must also be dying.

July 14, 1865. Thy ways are indecipherable, oh Lord. Ten men have we buried, committing their souls to the brighter world above, their bodies to the earth. We would have buried more had it not been for the brave action of one of the savages we came here to battle and yet the penalty remains a whipping for demonstrations of kindness towards our enemy. We hear of the merciless scalpings and innocent families slaughtered along the banks of the Snake River but in this land of nothing, of plants which root not in the ground but in wind and yield not, not beauty, not nutrition, we see all of your children struggling equally to survive – the Spanish, the Indian, the White Man – none with the strength to inflict a slaughter on the other. Many of the men are anxious to leave this place and return to battle the Yankees, an enemy well fed and armed sufficiently for a noble battle. But the Colonel insists the savage will arise and so we must stay.

I still suffer some of the effects of the influenza which held me in delirium these past weeks. My recovery is aided in no small part by the ointment provided by the savages. The smell is most foul but one application and peaceful sleep is upon me, thus my appetite grows. This morn I had recouped sufficiently to lead a small band of troops into a pleasant valley north of here where a few hearty souls raise cattle and potatoes for supplies. The men were most appreciative for a respite from their diet of beans, rice and rabbit—enjoying a side of beef roasted over an open pit and potato bread with great relish. They were also greatly cheered by news of a saloon opening for business in one of the many small mining settlements springing up on the sides of hills and mountains. Colonel Palmer will not be pleased. The miners have brought with them many vices—saloons and women of ill-repute; their insatiable lust for gold leads to an increase in stagecoach robberies, however, the men require some pleasures. SO

The last entry was written not as prose, but rambling poetry:

Written in the Shortening of Days . . .
Hail Osceola,
I have black toe
I have heard a whisper over the desert and know it calls my name.
By the ocean below the caves,
Where hidden under ice eternal,
The great mystery prevails.
Call me by the name I do not yet deserve,
That I might claim it on the other shore,
Lead me.
Feed my soul.
Else, devour me and I be nevermore.
The passing of the moon have I languished in the stockade,
fed once a day and left to sweat away my "mutinies."
Finally through the tender mercies of Small Owl
Am I reunited with pen and paper.
Should this record of Lonely Eagle survive
kindly return it to the banks of the Echoing waters,
In the crystal caves of Osceola,
Father come to us
Mother come to us
Brother come to us
Bring us back our bows
So shall we be led the way.

Past this entry were pages full of gibberish. A young officer, locked away for some reason, slowly going mad or perhaps he had gone mad and then been locked up. Or, perhaps it was a well-crafted forgery, and I'd been duped and hog-tied again.

At lunch it was obvious the girls knew I had their treasure. Knew that I'd found it jammed under the mattress of one of the beds (along with a pack of cigarettes and a lighter), read it while they were retrieving cleaning supplies, and then locked it in the trunk of the Nova. They sat across a long particle board table in the dining barracks, casting stones with their eyes as Winnie Peterson explained to them with undisguised relief: "Miss Butters will be leaving us tomorrow. Her elderly aunt is sick and she has to return home to take care of her."

"Don't you know it's a sin to steal?" Leticia snarled. Poor thing had a fresh outburst of zits, some of them bordering on boils, across her fragile cheekbones and on her forehead.

"What does that mean, Leticia?" Miss Peterson growled.

"She knows." Leticia hissed as four sets of blazing eyeballs threatened to burn holes through my skull.

"Miss Butters stole from you?"

"Why don't you tell Mrs. Peterson what you think I stole?" I asked.

"How ridiculous," Winnie Peterson snarled. "What would Dr. Butters want to steal from any of you? Quite frankly, I just don't have time for any of this! I have to move the four of you into different barracks. Meredith, starting tomorrow morning you and Leticia will bunk in Barracks 4; Thanh, you'll be in 2 and Bonny, 1. I've decided to put an end to this foolishness once and for all."

My, my. The tears they did flow, and from such tough lassies too. The award for biggest meltdown would have to go to Bonny, the longest in the system and the most full of psychobabble. She couldn't possibly be apart from Merry, her one and only friend in the whole messed-up world—it would force her further down the path to total mental insanity.

Apparently there are varying levels of insanity—from the mild, to the severe, and finally, to the total.

"Really Bonny. You're being released in—what is it—three months? I seriously doubt—"

"Miss Peterson, I've got abandonment issues, you just ask the therapist. I gotta be with Merry; I just gotta. I'm gonna live with her once we get out of here!"

Ah, the crux of the issue. Bonny had found a mark in the sweet-natured daughter of a wealthy and powerful man. Even in a khaki prison-girl uniform, Meredith Hyman had—as Fitzgerald would say—a voice full of money, exuding the promise of a brighter, greener world. She would always be a hustler magnet and Bonny, despite her innocent chocolate brown eyes, was a streetwise hustler.

Next up to bat was Thanh. "I can't be separate from Merry," she cried. "Other girls call me 'gook.' Hit me because I Vietnamese! And at home they beat me; tell me I'm ugly and useless. Merry take care of me."

Ha, I chuckled to myself, another future member of the Doug Hyman Home for Wayward Girls. Won't he be thrilled?

Of course their pleas were ignored; their requests denied. They were told to "put a sock in it" or risk KP duty. Miss Peterson had no more time to waste. It was movie time! Yahoo! And the movie this week? The Road to Rio.

"Hope and Crosby, Miss Peterson?" I chortled as she rose to set up the projector. (She was apparently the only adult at the facility trusted to run the thing.) "I hope you're planning on passing out valium! How many of these girls are going to enjoy watching men their grandfather's age massacre the art of the double entendre while tripping the light fantastic?"

She just stared at me as if I'd lost my mind. But I couldn't stop laughing. It was so damned ridiculous. Showing Hope and Crosby movies to a room full of incarcerated teens!

"You know, there is one thing funky about that movie. Right in the middle of their lame-brain cruise some Carmen Miranda type sings the little cockroach song."

"Why is that in any way odd?"

"Course they sing it in Portuguese, so no one knows what they're saying, still—do you think it was meant to be a subliminal message?"

"As usual, I have no idea what you're talking about," Winnie scowled. The projector was not behaving itself. The spools refused to thread properly, and the natives were getting restless.

"You know, Hope was famous for lampooning the anti-communists. Maybe he was snubbing his nose at McCarthy:

The cockroach says she has seven skirts of tulle.

It's a lie, she has one. Ah ra ra, go ro rho.

She has just one! The cockroach says she has a velvet shoe.
It's a lie, her foot is hair. Ah ra ra, go ro rho."
I'd gotten the attention of the Days of the Week.

"A cockroach wearing skirts?" Merry asked. "That doesn't make sense."

"The cockroach is a code name," I explained. "You see, the Spanish invaded Mexico hundreds of years ago and forced the natives to become Catholic. Any native speaking out against the Spanish authority would be punished, so they started making up nursery rhymes and songs about the cockroach and what a vile insect she was and how she would someday be chased out of the house, figuring that the Spanish would just think they were singing harmless children's songs."

"That's dumb." Bonny snarled. "Really dumb."

"Is it? Say you girls were plotting to overthrow Miss Peterson. You couldn't go around singing, Off with Miss Peterson's head. You'd have to make up a code name for her—like, say, Weasel. And then a code name for yourselves—say, Monkey. All around the mulberry tree, the monkeys chased the weasel. The monkeys escaped from the house, pop goes the weasel."

"Dr. Butters! What does that have to do with the movie they're about to see?" Winnie Peterson fired back as she finally got the projector to work. "Rio isn't in Mexico. It's in Brazil."

"Oh, I don't know. I just thought I'd give them a little background on the song—so when they heard it sung in Portuguese, they'd have some idea what was being sung," I paused for dramatic effect. "Weren't you ever curious why two staunch patriots like Hope and Crosby included a communist manifesto in one of their fluffy road movies?"

"Never! I've never heard such nonsense!"

CHAPTER 8

I DID NOT HAVE A PLAN. No, I did not. In fact, I kept reminding myself that I wasn't being paid to watch ninety minutes of Hope and Crosby with a barracks full of girls who thought a double entendre was an extra large meal. In fact, I wasn't getting paid at all unless you count the fact that I got to keep my job. Whoop-de-do! I could return to Vegas on the very next stage and report to Sheriff Hyman that all was hunky-dory up in Enev City. I imagined what I would say to him.

Butters to Hyman:

What we have here, your Worshipfulness is a group of young lassies, hormones raging to beat the band, who found an old journal and became enamored of its author—a gallant young cavalry officer whose writing is so poetic that, heck, I'm half in love with him! Driven by lust, they figured out a way of knocking out their dim-witted counselors (me included) so they could presumably track down the mysterious caves of Osceola and return the sacred journal to the banks of Echoing Waters. It's all just so romantic I could cry; how about you?

Ha, I chuckled, wouldn't it be a gas to watch Hyman wince at that story! To see him look up at me with disbelief, you gotta be kidding sprawled across his face. It might, just might, compensate for two days spent in the middle of nowhere. But, as silly as Hyman might consider girlish infatuations, the fact that his daughter was a red-blooded female lusting after a man (albeit a dead man) and not a lesbian devil worshipper would wag his inner Hef, getting me off the hook. I could hand the journal over to Winnie Peterson and, if it was indeed genuine, let her have the honor of donating it to the local historical society for preservation in a dusty, rarely visited museum where, under glass, his story would remain a mystery; where every now and then a vacationer might stop briefly to admire his beautiful penmanship, lamenting she had not the time to read the words, there being too many other relics to peruse and a martini waiting back at the hotel.

But to tidy up the case then and there, ambling off into the sunset, would have all the satisfaction of eating just one Cheeto. I had to know more. Such as, where had they found the journal and how had they managed to knock me out? They might be up to something dangerous.

It didn't take long for the antics of our onscreen nincompoops, Hot Lips (Hope) and Scat (Crosby), to put half the room to sleep and the rest to groaning, especially when Hot Lips and Scat realize they'd been hypnotized—a plot twist designed to artlessly cram more silliness into a plotline that already included a wicked stepmother, the Brazilian cavalry, and papers containing words so evil that Bob Hope tells the camera, "The world must never know." I had to get out of the room before I screamed.

Once outside in the bright yet cold air, I realized what I really needed was a comfy sofa to wiggle my rump into, a good book to digest, and a decent cup of tea flavored with honey and smelling as exotic as it tasted: orange blossoms, ginger and a dash of jasmine. But instead, I decided to check out the old cemetery behind Palmer House. Teenagers are always fascinated with cemeteries, death, and black clothes. There are all sorts of theories about why teenagers go through this phase, the most commonly accepted being that they are mourning the death of their childhood, a concept I pondered as I wandered up the hill unnoticed by anyone, or so I thought.

The cemetery gate was only four feet high, warped by age, and falling from its hinges. First it fell toward me and then away. Finally I wiggled it open far enough that I could awkwardly insert myself into the graveyard, all the while feeling as though I was being watched and I was, by the middle-aged senora in charge of housekeeping in Palmer House. Dios Mio. The crazy woman from Vegas is entering the graveyard. I waved at her. She crossed herself vehemently and then disappeared beyond the fluttering curtain like a scene in a Hitchcock film.

The graves were laid out in several rows of approximately twenty headstones each, some partially shaded by struggling oaks. The oldest graves were in front and dated from the 1880s—two decades after the cavalry had given up their quest for glory. In the bright sun, the sand-eroded inscriptions were nearly impossible to decipher. Further on, clusters of gravestones seemed to mark an era. An era of the McEnery family clustered under one of the healthier oaks:

McEnery, Bertha, b. 26 Jan 1890, d. 08 Mar 1890
Budded on Earth to bloom in Heaven

McEnery, George Henry, d. 15 Jul 1890, age: 10m 6d
We part dear one to meet in a brighter world above

McEnery, Sarah, b. 9 Mar 1826, d. 8 Nov 1899
Mother, A precious one
Mom is gone.
Advice we loved is stilled.
A place is vacant in our home.
Which never may be filled.

Many tombstones had been damaged and lay forlorn and neglected in the dust, the only flowers memorializing the dead, tumbleweeds, hundreds of them, blown in by the storm and now trapped by the fence. When I was a child, I thought the tumbleweed lived off air and was about the most useless plant ever invented by God. But later I learned the tumbleweed was just a plant with a bad plant habit. Plants afflicted by this bad habit refuse to die in the normal manner; their roots rot first allowing them to break away for a wild ride across the desert and through towns—traveling in gangs of other bad plant habits who refuse to go gentle into that good night, attacking moving cars, big rigs and trains. They are every bit as dangerous as locusts who decide to commit seppuku on the highway, but when trapped against a cemetery fence, the rebel tumbleweed resembles a pile of skeletal rib cages.

I was trying to read the inscriptions on the decaying wooden markers at the far end of the graveyard when I heard someone calling my name. Miss Butters, Miss Butters. It was Thanh. She looked shipwrecked, poor thing, panting as though she'd been running up the hill.

"Hey kid. Why so glum?" I asked as she bent over to catch her breath.

"Bonny has visitor—caseworker. Merry go with her."

"And Leticia?"

"I dunno. Saturdays we allowed phone call but I no want to call home. They call me useless trash."

"So you decided to come up and snoop around the graveyard with me? Perhaps find your Major Olivore."

"Major Olivore not here. Dead not honored here."

"He's not? Then where is he?"

"Echoing waters."

"Oh yeah," I chuckled. "How do you get to this Echoing waters?"

"I don't know. I only here three days."

"Do the other girls?"

"They have map."

Aha. I knew there were pages missing from the journal. "Where did they find his journal? Up here at the graveyard?"

She pulled strands of jet black hair out of her eyes and pointed to a ridge about a hundred yards up the mountain, beyond the fence. I asked how they'd gotten there—short of sprouting wings and flying. That's when she showed me. Ah, how easily they'd led me right into their trap again. The little shits.

CHAPTER 9

"IT'S THE NOVA LADY, Cal! I wonder what happened to her."

The speaker stood directly over me shining a bright red light into my face. I was floating through a universe of veins and pounding orbs, afraid to find out if my mortality had run out, when something cold and oily dropped onto my bare neck. It rolled between my clavicles and then ran over the edge of my neck and presumably to the ground, leaving a slime trail as it did. The smell – ah yes, the smell of that goo was enough to raise the dead.

The light pivoted, as I was examined from the other side, "Yup, it's her. She sure does show up in the darnedest places."

"Think it's a coincidence?"

"In the magical universe there are no coincidences and there are no accidents. Nothing happens unless someone wills it to happen," I interjected. "William Burroughs on the subject of coincidences— happy and otherwise." My body felt as though it had been put through a meat grinder, but the mouth still worked: "Whoever you are, would you kindly not shine your light directly in my face so I can open my eyes?"

"She's alive!"

"Quite possibly, but I may have broken something, and I'd prefer not to be blinded as well. Where am I anyway? The morgue?"

"She's alive and kicking," one of them joked as he backed off, and the world grew grey. I opened my eyes. Above me hung a forest of stalactites, lit bubblegum pink by the lanterns my rescuers held. Slowly I remembered slipping like a silly goose on a piece of oily shale and sliding down the old mine shaft, faster and faster as the ground became increasingly wet, reaching out to stop my slide only to accomplish a change in direction that propelled me out of the shaft and into a black hole. My fall must have been softened by the mushy surface on which I lay.

Carefully I checked my extremities, wiggling toes and fingers while rising to my elbows. All seemed well. "Where are your cowboy boots, gents," I chuckled, as they helped me to my feet. They were outfitted like deep-sea divers—spotlights on their helmets, safety goggles obscuring their eyes, and knee-high mud boots.

"You can't wear cowboy boots working down here in these caves."

"Then I presume you two are caveologists?"

They exchanged looks. "Yes. Caveologists. We work for the Lamarckian Echolocation Cultivation Theory Administration, or as we like to say, LECTA."

"LECTA, huh? Let me guess - Agriculture department?"

They nodded. Somehow the name LECTA sounded familiar but my head hurt too much for any complicated processing of data, "Well, if you could just show me how to get the hell out of here, I'll be much obliged and you can go back to your caveology activities."

"What are you doing down here in the first place? These caves are government property. We have to take you in for a 2-8-9 at HQ, don't we, Cal?"

"Oh, for pity's sake. I'm in here quite by accident. One of the inmates at Enev was about to show me how she and her buddies have been fleeing the coop when I fell—or was pushed—down an old mine shaft."

"We don't know that, Ma'am. First we run into you on Big Gulch Road and now down here. How can we be sure you're not a spy for BLM?"

"Luke, does she look like a spy for BLM?" Cal interjected. "This is a matter for Fearless Leader to decide. Remember our Code."

Spies, Fearless Leader, the Code – these guys sure were a hoot. I decided to play along with their game: "Earthlings, take me to your Leader."

"See – she's a wacko."

"I have a message from the planets of the confederation that can only be relayed to the earthling known as Fearless Leader. Klaatu barada nikto."

"Lady, you are weird."

"That's a ten-four. No hurry, but this message must be delivered before the Mars-conjunct-Jupiter; otherwise the systematic destruction of Planet Earth will commence."

"Very funny, lady—we'll get you out of here. Think she can make it up R 13, Cal?"

"I dunno. Can you rock climb, Ma'am?"

"Rock climb? Doesn't this cave have an entrance?"

"We can't take you out the entrance—it's top secret. You'll have to follow us."

"I forgot to tell you that I am level four classified on all secret caves but unfortunately my ID was lost when I fled in the escape pod."

"Then I guess, lady," Cal laughed, "you'll be climbing your way out. No proof of level four classification on secret caves means we've got to take you up the butt hole. Besides, that's where our truck's parked."

They led me through a stalactite forest, carefully calling my attention to deep ravines on either side of our trail. Below I heard running water, echoing against the stone wall like an organ in an ancient cathedral, and every now and then, the song of wings fluttering. Bats, the caveologist reported. That's what I'd landed in; what had probably saved my life—centuries of bat poop, now coating my backside. That's what had fallen on my neck; poop from their sample kits. Apparently the government had come up with a new use for the bat poop (top secret, of course).

Eventually we reached what appeared to be the end of the cave. There, against the cave wall, was a pile of boulders about twenty feet tall: damage done by blasting, I was told. On the other side of the wall was an old mine tunnel and — fresh air!

"All we have to do is climb up this pile and go through the hole."

"You're kidding," I chuckled.

"No big deal, lady," Cal explained. "Just follow me and Luke will spot you from behind."

"Spot me? I don't know how he can miss me."

"No, I mean, he'll catch you if you slip."

I took a good look at Luke. Late twenties, muscular but skinny. "If I slip, my advice to you, Luke, is to run for the hills," I warned.

"Don't worry, Ma'am. Luke and I were Navy Seals," Cal promised as he bounded up the rocks like a monkey. Not so me. I had all the strength of a Raggedy Ann doll. Everything hurt and Luke was no help. Every now and then, disgruntled by my caution, he put his bony hands on my ample derriere and pushed me upward like I was a cow he was trying to dislodge from a creek bed.

The butt hole was actually a small slit in the cave wall through which—they informed me (with straight faces!)—I was expected to squeeze.

"What do you think I am? A tube of toothpaste?"

"Come on, lady. We're almost there. You just need to slither through the hole like this," Luke ordered, removing his backpack and attaching it to his foot with a cord. Then he flopped onto his belly and, imitating a crocodile, disappeared into the rock wall, dragging his gear behind him.

"Your turn," Cal calmly informed me.

I got down on my hands and knees and started crawling towards the slit, "How long is this tunnel?"

"Only about twenty feet. Lady—get your rump down," he ordered, putting his boot on my butt. "Get down on your elbows and slither forward like a snake."

I hadn't slithered since I was eight. What if the opening wasn't big enough and instead of slithering through like the two GI Joes, I got stuck? Bring in the winch and pulley, boys. We've got a supersized pickle stuck down here.

"Slither, lady, slither," Luke urged, shining a light in my face from the other side.

"I'm slithering as fast as I can slither, gents!" I complained as I swam mostly on my belly over rock and dust, ripping my jeans to shreds and eating more dust than I displaced.

"Praise be to God and Allah and Buddha," I effused as we exited the bowels of the earth into the brilliant coral and gold of the setting sun. "Isn't life wonderful?"

"You can't believe in both God and Allah," Cal informed me coldly. The gents were busy disrobing, stripping off their headgear and heavy boots and tossing them in the back of their truck. We were on the edge of the mountain, looking out over a valley that appeared to have a trail of vegetation running through it, perhaps from a mountain-fed stream. Down the hill from the mine entrance were the ruins of a few wood structures, a small mining settlement gone bust no doubt.

"Right," I replied. "You're absolutely right. Thank you, Fod and Hal. Say, where are we?"

"Can't tell you that, Ma'am. In fact we're going to have to put blindfolds on you now and take you back to HQ for your 2.8.9."

"Is that right? Where are your badges? Your ID? Any sort of paper authorizing you to detain someone?"

"Let me put it to you this way, Ma'am. It's 7:00 pm and it'll be dark real soon. We can point you in the general direction of the prison but I've got to tell you, it's about a —I dunno, what would you say, Luke—two mile hike up and over those ridges and there ain't no path. Or you can come with us."

"Yeah," Luke chortled. "You gotta ask yourself, lady. Do you feel lucky?"

Chapter 10

WHY IS IT THAT YOUNG MEN always drive around with their dirty laundry piled in the back of their cars waiting to get lucky (and not in the way you're thinking): lucky to stumble upon a motherly type who'll happily bleach their dingy tees white again, while cooking them homemade macaroni and cheese? From the look of things in the truck, Cal and Luke hadn't gotten lucky in quite some time. Dirty tee shirts, socks, and empty fast-food containers littered the cramped cab.

"You gents ever hear of a laundry basket?" I complained as they wrapped an old rag around my head (my blindfold) and stuffed me in back with the debris.

"Just shove Luke's skivvies on the floor, lady—hey, what's your name?" Cal asked.

"Lady Annabella DuPont La Rosa," I told them, "and I don't touch men's dirty skivvies."

"Really?"

"Really."

"I don't suppose you have any identification."

"Nope. As I told you, I didn't intentionally drop into your bat cave. My wallet and my car are back at Enev. If you'd like to drive me over there, I can show you my ID, and then we can go to your headquarters where for a cheese sandwich I'll tell you whatever you need to know."

"Nice try, Lady La Rosa, but no way."

"Think we should go 'cross the desert?" Luke asked. "Or the highway? Highway's faster."

"Highway," I pleaded.

"We got a woman with a blindfold on in the back seat—what do think Einstein?"

"Desert."

"Yup."

"Can she take it?"

"Seems like a tough broad to me."

"A tough broad with glass kidneys!" I interjected. "So I hope you brought along something for me to pee in, 'cause I'm not squatting behind a sagebrush."

Cal was silent for a moment and then ordered: "Easy on the four-wheeling, Luke." But that command either fell to deaf ears or was impossible considering the terrain we were crossing. Indeed, after a few miles of jolting bumps and turns, I felt exceedingly grateful to be pillowed by the sweaty rankness of young men's dirty clothing. So grateful that I lay my head against a wadded towel, closed my eyes, and tried to assuage the irritation I felt at being waylaid by these two ignoramuses with a bit of deep-breathing and Transcendental Meditation. I tried to conjure a calming scene—a tranquil mountain lake or the endless sky. But alas, the only image offered by sleep-deprived cranial synapses was Bob Hope, mouthing "The world must never know" into the camera. Like a song you hate, spinning in an endless loop, a case of mental hiccups that can't be relieved by any measure, "The world must never know." Of course, the constant gibberish over the cowboy's two-way radio did not help my attempts at oneness with the universe.

"Sebbeth odremin nalla far, emos—correctess?"

Quiet. Then again: "Sebbeth odremin nalla far, emos—correctess?"

"Hell, what's he saying now, Cal?"

"Why ask me? I don't even know what he's saying when he's talkin' normal and not in the stupid code."

The radio cackled on again: "Wholeo lefnear?"

"Christ Almighty. What do we say?"

"Let me handle this, Luke," Cal replied. "Artemis: Fox and Birddog are coming in for a landing and they're carrying trout."

"Trout?" I giggled. "I'm a trout?"

"That's our code word for intruder."

"I see Who do you think is overhearing your conversation— other than me and I'm in the backseat and know very well that I've got the bloody hook in my mouth?"

"The BLM, lady. And we don't think; we know."

"I see. So one branch of the government is spying on another?"

They were quiet for a few seconds, apparently exchanging glances, and then Luke said with John Wayne inflection: "The less you know, the better, Ma'am."

"That's a downright silly statement considering you're dragging me back to your secret hangout where I'm bound to learn more than I already know now. Wouldn't it be better just to drop me off outside of Enev and hope that any story I tell will be laughed off? I mean, it is kind of silly."

"We got our orders."

"Now gents, there's a phrase that should be flat-out censored from the English language, unless, of course, you're at a fast food place: We got our orders. It ends a conversation and closes a mind faster than a speeding bullet. It tight-lips the tight-lipped and leads the Custers of the world to their Waterloos."

"Lady, do you ever stop?"

"We put the gag around the wrong part of her face, Cal," Luke chuckled as he downshifted. We seemed to be climbing back up the side of the mountain, and then abruptly we stopped.

The man they called Fearless Leader had a felonious cackle, "You blindfolded her, but you didn't tie her hands?" He laughed after I'd been led from the truck into what amounted to little more than a giant tin can, reeking of burnt coffee and fried electronic parts.

"I had my eye on her the whole time, Dr. Gnecht," Cal reported as he removed the rag from around my head.

The aforesaid Dr. Gnecht didn't bother to stand in greeting but just sat behind a worn desk looking up at me through thick lenses. Behind him, a computer mainframe and a shortwave radio buzzed. The cavelike feeling of the trailer was amplified by plastic, wood-grained paneling, and thick shag carpeting which had at one time been a putrid shade of green but now was polka-dotted by coffee stains and God knows what else.

"I'm Dr. Gnecht, Lamarckian Echolocation Cultivation Theory Administration. Boys, it's practically dark outside—don't you think the blindfold was overkill?"

"This lady keeps showing up everywhere—yesterday she was snooping around on Big Gulch Road."

"Since when is it a crime to get lost on a desert road? Oh, I get it—Big Gulch Road leads to this place, doesn't it?" I inserted.

"What were you doing in my caves?" he asked, ignoring my question.

At that point, I'd had enough. "You know, I don't really give a rat's ass what you're doing. I don't even care if you're teaching bats to fly! I'm hungry as hell and I smell like Satan's fart. I demand you let me call a taxi, or take me back to Enev."

"Who are you?" Gnecht demanded.

"I work at Enev as a counselor but only for another day and then I'm quitting. I've had enough of smart-mouthed teenagers."

"Ha, I wonder where they learned to be smart mouths!" Cal chuckled. "She says there's an old mine shaft on the grounds of Enev, and that's how she fell into the caves."

"Listen, Dr. Whoever You Are, the first thing I intend to do is to tell the superintendent, Ms. Peterson, about that mine. Besides giving the little brats an escape route, it's a bloody safety hazard! I'm sure it will be sealed up before you can say lickety-split."

"No one must ever know about the caves!" Gnecht hissed. "No one!"

"Oh for Pete's Sake! What the hell makes you think anyone at Enev—particularly a group of fifteen-year-old girls—is at all interested in your bat-poop project, and, by the way, where the hell is the paperwork that gives you any legal right to ask me these questions, let alone detain me?"

Gnecht grimaced: "We're not detaining you. As soon as we know where the opening is, we'll take care of it. The world must never know—at least not yet."

There it was again, that phrase: the world must never know. The world must never know. I was losing my mind.

"You think the three of you are going to be able to break into a state penal facility and seal up a mine shaft without anyone noticing? Why don't you just try bribing the superintendent? She seems bribable."

"You certainly are a smartass, lady. Are you sure you're a prison counselor?"

"As sure as I am that Cal and Luke here are caveologists."

"Caveologists." He snorted, giving his cohorts a sideways glance and roll of the eye.

"She said at least one of the girls knows where the entrance is," Cal interrupted, reiterating what I thought he had just said. "They've been using it to escape from Enev."

"It's the entrance to an old mine they're using, not the cave. For Pete's sake! I fell about twenty feet from the mine shaft into the cave—if the girls were doing the same thing, don't you think you would have run into them by now—lost in the dark and crying their eyes out? Speaking of which, I hate to interrupt the interrogation, but by now someone at Enev is bound to have noticed I'm missing. You'd better let me use one of those mobile phone thingies to give them a call."

He ignored my request, instead staring at my face as though I had suddenly sprouted horns. I'd seen the look before in multiple personalities. It was the doorbell announcing a new arrival to the body. Ding, dong, Doris coming through. In all other ways, Gnecht reminded me of grad students I'd known, so eager for honors that they latched onto any and all extra credit assignments, even those designed for the struggling students. The kind of nerdy kid you try to make friends with because he has no friends— and then you find out why.

I withstood the intense scrutiny of my asymmetrical features as long as I could, "Excuse me, but do I have a face you can't resist memorizing or . . ."

Gnecht continued staring. Then he muttered. "No, I don't think she has it. Are you listening?" He wasn't talking to me. And he wasn't talking to Cal or Luke.

We were waiting to hear what Gnecht would do or say next when a sharp crackle broke the stillness, followed by a second and a third.

The men froze.

"Sounds like someone nearby is shooting up beer bottles for fun," I chuckled. "Though it seems a little silly to start target practice in the evening!"

The next shot blew out the back window of Luke's truck.

"Holy smoke!" I shouted, dropping to the carpet. I was followed by Cal and Luke. Someone was using the Airstream for target practice.

"Take care of it," Dr. Gnecht ordered, rather calmly I thought for a man being shot at.

"Our guns are in the truck!"

"Why hell, no wonder you're on the floor," Gnecht growled. "I'll have to take care of it my damned self!" He pulled a revolver from the desk and stepped over our prostrate bodies. Swearing under his breath, he opened the door and began firing. "Get out of here, you damned old buzzard!" he shouted as he continued firing. A horse whinnied in the distance, and then all was quiet.

"Get off the damned floor, you two morons. Take care of that guy, but don't hurt the horse!"

The "boys" scrambled to their feet and were gone in seconds, leaving me alone with Gnecht.

"Shouldn't you call the police?" I suggested.

He was built like a pipe cleaner and about as attractive, but not very tall, maybe five-seven. It was hard to guess his age; his unkempt, shoulder-length hair was speckled with grey, but his face was unlined, his chin, prickly as though he intended to grow a beard when he grew up.

"Ha! We take care of ourselves out here. Besides," he explained, "we know who he is."

"Disgruntled employee?"

"Let's go," he blurted out, ignoring my question.

"Where are we going?" I asked.

"I'm taking you back to Enev."

I was tempted to question his abrupt about-face but the rule of thumb when dealing with armed and unstable schizophrenics is to question them in public places and not alone in an Airstream trailer far out in the desert. Know what I mean?

"I shouldn't take time from my work," he complained as he led me to a banged-up Jeep. "But you can't be here any longer. You'll contaminate everything—set me back months. Caveologists, shit, is that what those two idiots told you they were? It's amazing what's coming out of grad school these days. You would have thought— considering the importance of my research they would have sent me—at the very least!—students well versed on inherent evolutionary patterns. But, NO. Instead I get a couple of Ivy League yahoos with boot fetishes. You know one of those idiots was actually afraid of my bats? Incredible. Get in the car, lady!"

When the moon shines on the desert floor, it reflects off a dry surface of mica, silica, and chalk, producing its own atmosphere in which all things appear ashen and bloodless, like the dead surface of an alien planet. It's an illusion. There's actually quite a lively world on the desert floor, comprised of crawling, slithering, and short-hopping night creatures fluttering from one event to another like Saturday night partygoers in Manhattan. It's not really a party; it's a hunt. Every now and then, there's a squeal or a howl, as you realize party time has ended for some poor creature.

As we drove along, Gnecht unloaded tidbits about himself that were hardly a surprise: he was misunderstood (of course) and grossly unappreciated by scientists not worthy to say his name in public, let alone work beside him. If my situation weren't so tenuous, I would have yawned him off, although, I have to admit that I was intensely curious about his research. To a Lamarckian, bats would provide ample proof of the necessity to mutate, however if I engaged him on this topic, he'd probably guess that I was not an ordinary prison counselor. Lamarck is not typically discussed, even in courses on genetics and evolution, in an undergraduate milieu. And so I bit my tongue and pressed away from the intellectual debate I would have loved to pursue; in fact, I managed to keep my mouth shut for a good many miles, and then I had to ask, "Have you found the body yet?" It was not my smartest move.

CHAPTER 11

"I CAN'T LET YOU GO to the police with that theory." Gnecht hissed, his hands strangling the poor steering wheel. We'd just turned onto the highway, which gave me hope that he did not intend to do away with me and leave my body in a gully for the jackals and creepy crawlies to dine upon.

"I understand the need to keep your research confidential. But she's got relatives anxious to know what happened to her."

"She's not down in the caves! You're the only one they allowed to find the caves."

"Why me?" I ventured. "Why did they let me in?"

"You have epiphysis cerebri."

"What?"

"Epiphysis cerebri – the third eye. Look."

He pulled down the visor and invited me to take a gander at my face. Nose, too large. Lips like a bow. Eyes, short-lashed and dark brown, but alas—only two stared back at me, not three.

"I only see two eyes, a misshaped nose, and Kewpie-doll lips. No third eye."

"See the indentation up and between your brows. Yours is inactive, of course, which is why you had to leave. The inactive epiphysis cerebri is unstable and, instead of producing the harmonious rhythms, can disturb delicate ecosystems. Of course, they can't tell the difference, which is why you were allowed in but you can't stay."

The poor man had been exploring bat caves for too long. "I have heard that bats are extremely sensitive to their environments . . ."

"Bats? You think I'm talking to the bats? I'm not crazy—it's you and all the other people like you. Why am I doing this? Why?" He hissed, skidding to a stop on the highway.

The move took me by surprise. Butters, you better cut the sarcasm, I told myself. Proceed as though you're dealing with someone about to launch himself into a full blown paranoid psychosis.

"That's who I assumed you were talking about, the bats. Who else lives down in the caves?"

"Ha! Wouldn't you like to know—wouldn't everybody like to know."

"I'm sure they would but . . ."

"Get out of the car."

"What?"

"Get out of the car! I've got to get back—I've been away too long. They'll get confused! They're already upset with me."

"You can't just leave me out here."

"Don't treat me as if I'm stupid. I know you're wired. The Bureau probably knows exactly where we are," he spat, gazing out into the dark desert. "They're probably even watching us as we speak!"

"Who? Who's watching us?"

"Don't play the innocent with me. It's the BLM, isn't it?"

"I promise you—I don't work for the Bureau of Land Management. There's no one watching us. No one knows where I am except you—just drive me to the next town at least! You can't leave someone on the side of this highway at night."

"Ha—you won't be alone for long. They'll come and pick you up, now that they know your cover is blown. Get out now!" He snarled, pushing and kicking me with his boots until I stumbled from the car. "Tell them, better luck next time."

I stood stunned as he U-turned in front of me and roared back in the direction from which we'd come. I couldn't move. This couldn't be happening, I thought. It was a dream or a nightmare. There was not a speck of light on either horizon. Overhead the stars' icy glare made me feel like the smallest most insignificant, stupidest blob of protoplasm in the universe. Why had I even brought up the subject of the missing counselor? I knew I was dealing with a man with more than a few loose screws. If I'd just kept my big mouth shut, but no, not me. Not Big-Mouthed Fi.

At first I convinced myself it might not be that dire of a situation. If Dr. Gnecht's headquarters were at the end of Big Gulch Road then the old man's store couldn't be more than four or five miles down the highway. Confidently I set off in what I hoped was the right direction. South. Or was it South? The moon was directly overhead making it difficult to locate the Little Dipper. If only I'd paid more attention in my astronomy classes.

I'd had patients who traveled vast distances, climbed foreboding mountains—all for the experience of complete quiet, that existential moment in which you feel your aloneness and also your connection to the eternal. I'd listened to them as they told me about the sense of awe and revelation they'd felt when all alone under the stars, feeling the vastness of the universe and their own insignificance, and then I had told them I felt the very same way curled up reading a book in the library. Wide-open spaces, abandoned of life, only left me with a sense of dread. Not the ordinary monster-under-the-bed dread but the certainty that there waited beyond this life only timeless emptiness. From a professional standpoint, I had analyzed my agoraphobia forward, backward, and six ways to Sunday. It was guilt. The irrational poltergeist all of us carry for something we did or didn't do.

There was only one thing to do. Sing.

"I'm Henery the Eighth, I am," I warbled as I shuffled along. It was the only song I could remember all the lyrics to.

Henery the Eighth, I am, I am.

I got married to the widow next door and

She was married seven times before and

Every one was a "Henery."

She wouldn't have a Willy or a Sam.

No Sir! I'm 'er eighth old man, I'm "Enery,"

Henery the Eighth I am.

Second verse same as the first.

I'm Henery the Eighth, I am . . .

By the umpteenth round of Henery, my throat hurt and I still had not reached the store in Steptoe. I figured I'd been walking for about twenty minutes. The scenery hadn't changed, nor had a car passed or a comet scurried across the horizon. There was no sound of life other than an occasional shuffling through the sand which I hoped was the wind. It was then that the mother of all dreads hit me smack dab in the face: I could be heading in the wrong direction. My assumptions about Big Gulch Road could have been all wrong. Yup, instead of heading toward Steptoe, I was probably marching toward the longest stretch of nothingness from here to Vegas, like a swimmer out of sight of land heading out to sea instead of back towards shore. It was a grim moment, not to be cheered by any amount of singing. Should I turn around or keep going?

"Rats!" I shouted. "Poopy, fudgey, rats! I'm sick of this nonsense! Damned sick of it. Enough already. Where's the damn director for this ridiculous farce? Come out, come out, wherever you are, and shout CUT. It's time to move on to the next scene!"

Apparently I'm an atheist only during the day. Alone, on an abandoned highway at night, I'm a firm believer in whatever deity is willing to pull the switch and start the action. That's why a backstage life full of circus performers in perpetual motion all night long is perfect for me. Keeps me from being alone in the dark, something I'd had a problem with since my father's death, and now it was all coming back to me. That night with all its smells—gasoline mingled with gin, dusted with laundry detergent, blood. The bone-chilling cold when your blood pressure plummets and you go into shock. It was all coming back to me.

My father was as nice a drunk as you'd ever want to meet: a romantic and insatiable reader, but alas, a man with a head planted firmly in the stars. He died in the desert, leaving me alone. No matter how many times I'd tried to silence the reverberation of guilt I felt for the accident, jumping from one couch to another, meditating, medicating, confessing, primal screaming, and even acupuncturing, guilt is a disease like alcoholism; it can be controlled and managed but never completely cured.

"You caused the accident with your smart mouth," the voice of my ever-present inner child whispered.

"You little shit. That's not true."

It is perfectly OK to tell your so-called inner child that she's full of shit, although generally it's better to do so when in a therapy session (at least, that's what I used to tell my patients).

"See the star at the end of the handle of the Little Dipper, Fiona," Papa began as we drove from Reno to Salt Lake late one night. I was seven. (That's pretty much what I remember of my childhood—long drives across the state, being deposited at a grandmother's, an aunt's, a cousin's.) "That's the North Star. Unlike the other stars, it doesn't change position, and do you know what that means?"

Because I was his only child, he often overestimated my intelligence: "The other stars go around it like the sun?" I responded.

"Nooooo," he laughed, reaching for the bottle.

It hadn't been the first dive into the bottle. I blamed it—the bottle—for the fact that my mother was no longer around, for the fact that we didn't have a permanent home, and for the fact that I had no friends other than the encyclopedia. I made a wisecrack—some snide bit of slander I'd picked up from my acerbic grandmother. He reached over to give me a swat. The car went out of control. I woke up alone by the side of desert highway at night. End of the story. Now here I was again, twenty years later. Hell, I'd been a lot braver back then, or so it seemed.

I was so lost in trying to analyze my way out of intense and paralyzing anxiety that when I heard the sound of the car, I told myself it was a hallucination—that on top of everything else, I was hearing things. But then I saw two headlights bobbing towards me from the horizon. "Praise be to all the saints and saintresses! Thank you, oh mighty stage director in the sky!" I said aloud. I was saved.

I had a brief and sobering thought that it might be Dr. Gnecht or one of his boys, but luckily I could recognize the purr of an expensive sports car. Hubby number one (the only one, thankfully) was a man with a Ferrari appetite, a Volkswagen budget and a zipper that never could stay closed. The only thing I learned from him, besides the blessing of abstinence, was the sound of a Jag.

CHAPTER 12

I HAD LOST TOUCH with the casualness money lends to the enjoyment of luxury. My rescuer's Jaguar smelt of lavender, the eau de cologne for the enlightened set, with just the right hint of new leather. At first I declined to sit on the plush passenger's seat until she produced a towel. What a rank amateur I exposed myself to be! The privileged sink their dusty derrieres wherever they please, regardless of the resulting mess for the clean-up crew. Pardonne moi!

"I can't apologize enough for my smell. You certainly are a saint for even letting me into your car," I blathered, politely opening the window.

"What happened?" she asked. From her appearance I jumped to the unfair conclusion that she was a showgirl, on her way from Vegas to Jackson Hole or some such resort locale in a "friend's" jag. She had a dancer's endless legs, long blonde hair piled loosely on top of her head and a voice cooled by years of performing on a smoky stage. However, she was dressed in a simple white sari and wore little jewelry or makeup, so I allowed that I could be dead wrong about her profession.

Figuring I'd sound like a blithering idiot if I told her the truth, I lied. "My car broke down and the gentleman who offered me a ride to the next town turned out to be a lunatic with a bat fetish—hence my lovely aroma!"

"And he left you out here in the middle of nowhere?"

"Yup!"

"Wow."

"Well, apparently the little people in his head didn't like me. I guess it could have been worse—they could have told him to kill me!"

"Oh my God," she cried, shifting rapidly from first to second and then third as we blasted off. "What were you doing way out here in the middle of nowhere?"

"I work down the road at the Eastern Nevada Girls Training Facility?"

"Oh my God!" she breathlessly gasped. "I don't believe it—that's where I'm going!"

"What a happy coincidence for me."

"Rev. Achmed, my guru, says that there are no coincidences. Kindred souls ebb and flow together at certain preordained points, and we will for the rest of eternity!"

"Sounds like he's read Siddhartha a few times."

"Siddhartha?"

"Yeah – a book by Hermann Hesse. Say, do you know how to get to Enev?" The Jaguar was slicing through the night like a hot knife through butter—80, 90 even up to 95 miles per hour.

"Sort of—we turn off just past someplace called Cave Lake, right?"

"It depends on which way we're heading—if we're driving north the turnoff is just past the Steptoe exit."

"Oh, that was miles back. And we are going north."

"Aha."

"Then we should probably turn around. Right?"

"Yup."

"Hold on."

Slowing ever so slightly, she executed a burning rubber U-turn and then began tearing up the other lane of the highway.

"You know Enev's going to be locked up tighter than a drum by now," I shouted. "They might not let you in."

"What?" She shouted in return. We had to shout to overcome the wind noise from the open windows.

"They—might—not—let—you—in."

"Ha," the pretty woman laughed, "see the envelope on the back seat? It's a court order."

"You just passed a sign."

"Shit! What did it say?"

I rolled up the window. "Might I suggest that we drive a little bit slower? The signs on this highway are difficult to spot even in broad daylight. At night, they're impossible, especially driving at the speed of light."

"Sure," she agreed. "It's just the desert freaks me out, you know. It's so . . . I don't know—dead."

"Aye, that it is." I started to ask why she was on her way to Enev, when she cut me off, leaning forward into the windshield.

"What's that?" There were lights ahead on the right side of the highway. "I hope it's a gas station? I am a little low."

I wondered what she meant by "a little low" but was too afraid to ask. "I think it's the store at the Steptoe exit which means we've passed the road to Enev."

As we got closer, I realized the lights were not coming from the store but from the oversized truck with a blown-out back window parked in front. It was the truck belonging to Dr. Gnecht's cohorts, Luke and Cal. "Turn around," I ordered and she did.

CHAPTER 13

THE THIRD MRS. DOUG HYMAN, who now went by the name "Jasmine Morningstar", expressed barely guarded disappointment when the famous Dr. Fi Butters turned out to be the smelly woman she'd picked up by the side of the road. But because she'd been able to charm a judge in Reno into ordering her daughter Meredith released to an expensive psychiatric facility, she no longer really cared. She was curious, however, curious enough to listen as I explained to both her and Ms. Peterson why the old mine entrance needed to be sealed at once.

"Wow," she muttered, shifting uncomfortably in the metal chair. "When I was her age, I thought Elvis was some kind of god, but at least he was alive."

"Well, the girls evidently think Major Olivore was able to evade the Grim Reaper and now waits for them at the caves of Osceola. I'm sure it's just a phase they're going through—like a fascination with the occult. Course it doesn't help that they're with a bunch of other girls with no real-life boys to agonize over."

"We'll find the mine entrance tomorrow and seal it, if indeed it does exist." Ms. Peterson interrupted with an assurance aimed at the third ex-Mrs. Hyman, not me.

"Well then, that's great," I replied, "and now, since my services are no longer needed, I'll be on my way." It was nearly 10 pm, and I had just enough gas in the Nova to reach Pioche, a town rumored to have an all-night service station. With any luck I'd make it to Vegas by one or two in the morning, take a shower, and finally get some sleep.

"I'm leaving too," Mrs. Hyman reported. "As soon as I round up my Merry."

"And you complete the release of liability," Miss Peterson reminded her, as she readied a daunting pile of release paperwork, "and these other forms."

"And—you get someone to sell you some gas!" I chimed in. The Jag had sputtered to a complete stop about one hundred feet from the entrance to Enev and still sat outside the gate, useless. There being no gas station and only a few ten-gallon drums of low grade gas used for the emergency generators at the facility, she would have to convince one of the staff to let her siphon gas from the tanks of their own cars if she had any hope of getting anywhere that night. "If I were you, I'd spend the night here and have someone in Ely bring you out the high octane stuff in the morning. You'll blow out the engine of the Jag if you put rat-butt gas in it."

"Oh, I don't care," she said, "it's just a car. A possession. I can't stay here—the vibes are too strange."

"OK, suit yourself." The car must belong to Doug Hyman, hence disposable, I thought. I'd forgotten that in order to achieve Nirvana, you have to rid yourself of all possessions—even if it costs you or someone else a fortune. Nirvana ain't cheap.

Poor Ms. Peterson. First she'd been jolted from her nightly routine by our unscheduled and unorthodox arrival on-scene, then informed by court order that she was to release a girl forthwith (on a Saturday night! After hours!). And finally, to find out there was a mine shaft somewhere on the grounds of Enev. I hated to spring the worst on her, but it had to be done.

"If I were you, Miss Peterson, I'd have the police search the caves beneath the mine shaft before you seal it up. I hate to say it, but that's probably where you'll find the missing counselor. She may have followed the girls up there and fallen into one of the many crevasses."

"The police?"

"Yes. The police," I repeated. Was she considering not calling the police? "Listen Ms. P., I don't know who those bozos running around down there are, but I'm quite certain there is no department of the government called 'The Lamarckian Echolocation Cultivation Theory Administration.'"

"I don't even know what that means."

"Well, Lamarck was a French scientist who put forth a controversial theory on evolution, and echolocation refers to the ways bats communicate—what the two of them have to do with each other, I don't know and I don't care. All I know is they have guns and are extremely paranoid."

"Well, Dr. Butters, in this neck of the woods . . ."

"Yes, I know. That could describe half the people in these parts. But thanks to me, these particular idiots have their sights on your little facility."

Winnie Peterson picked up the phone, thought a second, and then put it back down again. "I can't call the county sheriff tonight. It's Saturday night. Stoney doesn't respond to nonemergencies on a Saturday night. And tomorrow, that's a Sunday—earliest he'd make it out here would probably be Monday."

"Then I'd suggest calling in any extra security folk you can."

"Oh, that's ridiculous. No one would try to break into a state prison."

She did have a point and so—giving myself permission not to give a damn what happened next—I said adieu to the two ladies. There's only so much you can do to save the world. I did know one person who could help. It was a long shot, but I decided I'd give it a try once I got home.

The Nova waited for me under the moonlight. Ah, freedom, I thought, as I fired up all two precious cylinders, and off we raced across the dry lake bed. I figured I'd keep the car for the night and then return it in the morning to the rental car place where my trusty steed (a fifteen-year-old Datsun truck) awaited me. That seemed the most logical re-entry to my well-ordered world. A lot of people accuse me of driving an old wreck in order to gain notoriety as a genuine eccentric, but you know, you don't have to worry about keeping an old car clean, or about where you park it, or who drives it.

For the first hundred miles I felt as free as a biker on a Harley. With his daughter no longer at Enev, Hyman wouldn't give a damn about me, and I could go back to my lowly but comfortable station as the Queen of Props. I knew by reputation the place Meredith Hyman was headed: a converted tubercular sanitarium in the Sonoma hills.

It was secluded, woodsy—the perfect place for a romantic like Meredith Hyman. In no time she'd find another Major Olivore, maybe even a living one. And the Major? I pictured his journal lying behind a glass counter, unread but preserved, like a zillion other testimonials to a life led, slowly turning to dust. Ah, the ultimate futility of art, I thought. Everything men have worked so hard to produce eventually turns to dust, everything. And then it dawned on me that I'd forgotten to give the journal to Ms. Peterson. It was still sitting in the trunk of the Nova. Suddenly I no longer felt free.

I can't explain what happened next. Lack of sleep, stress, that package of Hostess donuts I had in lieu of dinner—any and all could have contributed to the irrational thoughts that now floated through my head. I began to wonder if I'd formed a subconscious attachment to the journal, perhaps believing a romantic sensibility too soon taken from the world, like the pulsing heart removed from a still breathing elk, did not deserve an eternity in an obscure museum. But, if I kept it, what would I do with it? Put it in a fishbowl and tend it all day? I knew the publishing world well. If Major Olivore had been a nephew of Lincoln, run off with the black mistress of Robert E. Lee, fought Indians in the West, and founded Mormonism, then I might have a chance of getting publishers interested in his journal. Only might. A lot would depend on the whim of the public who might be more interested in a woman who has undergone multiple surgeries to look like Cher.

Now this next episode might seem silly to anyone who's gotten a good night sleep, a good meal, and a hot shower, but as I drove through the moonlit night, I began feeling like I wasn't alone. The journal of Sebastian Olivore became a living, breathing entity locked in my trunk. The more it breathed, the more evil it became, the more powerful, like an evil amulet, Sauron's ring of power, so shiny and beautiful that it could corrupt even Mother Teresa. Like Frodo, I must dispose of it. But where? The fires of Mordor? The tomb of King Tut? Doug Hyman's office? Maybe I shouldn't touch it at all. Maybe I should just leave it in the Nova, and let the rent-a-car people deal with it. No, that was a bad idea—that would just transfer the evil to another poor person.

What was left of my rational mind tried without success to interject a wee bit of sanity: In your exhausted state, you've ascribed evil powers to a diary. To a diary, Fi. Think about it. The journal has no power over you.

It didn't help. As soon as I got to Vegas, I decided, I was heading for the Excalibur. There had to be a Fire of Mordor someplace in that pink and blue medieval monstrosity. I'll take the journal and drop it into the fake fiery pit.

Luckily, before I wigged out any further, the all-night gas station in Pioche sprung from out of nowhere, landing smack dab in front of me on the highway, so brightly lit that it could be seen from outer space. Beside it was a sign welcoming visitors:

Welcome to Pioche: A living Ghost Town.

Once the roughest mining camp in the Old West, rougher than Tombstone and Dodge City! Seventy-two men died in gunfights before a natural death occurred. Visit Boot Hill and Murderer's Road! Have a Sarsaparilla at the Bucket of Blood!

I staggered around in the bright fluorescent light like a drunkard, gulping in dusty air and trying to get some blood flow to my numb feet and hands while the tank filled. Seeing another human—the cashier in his booth—brought me back from the Land of Mordor.

"Excuse me," I asked the cashier, a young man who looked up at me blankly, "but is this Bucket of Blood place still open? The desert's making me a little daft—I'm starting to have conversations with my alternate personalities! I could sure use a Sarsaparilla and some conversation."

"They close at 9. If you're thirsty there's a coke machine in back."

"Thanks. I guess Pioche is so dead that even the ghosts have left town," I chuckled. It was a joke he'd obviously heard one too many times or perhaps he actually was a ghost. It was hard to tell. He could have been one of the seventy-two gunslingers who had to die before there could be a natural death.

Once past the town founded on blood, the highway wound through hilly country for which I was eternally grateful. It kept me from falling asleep. But thirty minutes later it straightened out again, becoming a long straight strip of asphalt heading towards an eternally shifting horizon. Along the route, signs warned drivers not to spend too much time by the side of the road. What they should have read was: "Beware. Radioactive fumes. Hold Your Breath for the Next Fifty Miles." To the west lay the Nevada Atomic Test grounds. I was gliding along the sandy bed of an ancient ocean, now filled with the fossils of silvery radioactive fish flying over me. Once or twice, I joined them and swam above the speeding car. And then I returned, apparently not missed. The car was on such a straight path that a driver was an accessory.

An hour later the pastel dome over Vegas pulled a trick on my exhausted mind. For a frightening moment, I thought the sun was rising from the west, having spun around the earth in reverse. A certain sign of apocalyptic end of days. But it was only Vegas, the town that never sleeps. The empty two-lane highway flowed clumsily into the main truck route. "Welcome to Las Vegas," the sign read. Suddenly I was engulfed by a swarm of all-night truckers, sights clearly set on the all-you-can-eat breakfast buffets awaiting them, gunning their oversized rigs and threatening to overrun anything in their path, including me. A big fella on my bumper flashed his brights into my rearview mirror, blinding me. I sped up and attempted to change lanes but was cut off. I don't remember what happened next.

I awoke next to a ringing phone in a bright and sunny hospital room, a major pain in my head. The bed next to me was empty, but nurses were just outside.

"Hey!" I yelled, but they ignored me. The phone persisted in torturing me, until I knocked the receiver off the hook.

"Butters?" it squawked. "Butters, you there?"

"What?" I shouted back to the receiver.

"Blah, blah, blah," the voice mumbled.

"I can't hear you—I'm in a damn hospital bed!"

"Pick up the phone, Butters!" the voice insisted.

"Hell no! I'm injured!" Painfully I propped myself up to look for lower extremities. "Hot damn, I still have my legs and feet!"

"Don't be cute, Butters, I already checked with the hospital. You just have a concussion."

"Thank you, Dr. Hyman . . ."

"What did you say?" he growled.

"Nothing. Are you calling to wish me a speedy recovery?"

"Hell no. Pick up the phone, Butters—I'm tired of yelling at you!"

"Fire!" I screamed. That finally brought a nurse.

Chapter 14

AFTER HYMAN'S CALL, a friendly doctor informed me that I'd been in the hospital for two days, and that during those two days, I'd had moments of lucidity. I did not remember them, which led me to wonder if alternate personalities had been knocked loose during the accident. My other injuries were minor: a few lacerations, bumps, and bruises.

"Do you remember what you said yesterday?" one nurse asked. "You wanted to go to the circus."

"No."

"You were quite charming and funny," said the other.

"Really?"

"A pain in the rump," reported the doctor.

"That sounds more like me," I chuckled. "Alas, I don't remember any of the last two days. And sorry to say, I don't remember you, Doctor."

"Do you remember Ellen or Laura?" he asked, indicating the two nurses standing behind him. I sat up and looked at each of their faces. "Nope."

Post-traumatic anterograde amnesia was the prognosis. It could go on for weeks, months even. It could be mild (simply forgetting details) or it could be severe (don't ask). One moment you could be deeply engrossed in a murder mystery and the next, remember nothing of what you'd read. You could meet someone in the morning and forget them completely by evening. In this condition, the inflicted are doomed to have the ultimate Zen experience of living in the moment, whether they want to or not. There are drugs, of course; there are always drugs. And therapies, of course, there are always therapies.

"Should I wear a sign or something?" I asked the doctor. "You know—OUT TO LUNCH—that sort of thing, so people won't be upset when I forget who they are?"

"Doctor Butters—can I call you Doctor Butters?" he asked. He was an earnest sort who looked like Dennis the Menace's father.

"Sure, why not?"

"A couple of days ago you read me the riot act for calling you 'doctor.'"

"That was Trudy," I laughed. "She wouldn't have a Willy or a Sam. I'm her eighth old man, I'm 'Enery. Enery the Eighth, I am! Second verse, same as the first!'"

"This may take a while," Dennis the Menace's father chuckled. "I think we'll start her on a round of Dicsocort-a-mileathiapede for anxiety, and tell me, Dr. Butters, are you still constipated?"

"Do you think that the two conditions might be related?" I asked facetiously.

"You're the psychiatrist!" he laughed.

"Give me the prunes. If they bring back my short-term memory, I'll give you the AMA citation." That elicited a familiar laugh from the two nurses.

"I don't think we have stewed prunes on the menu. How about a suppository?"

I stuck my tongue out at him. He got the picture. I knew what I needed: an apple for the plumbing, and a bit of juggling for the old synapses, wiggling of the disjointed dendrites, mental pushups until my brain cells felt strong enough to write on that blackboard in my brain known as long-term memory. I did not to need to be enrolled in Experiments in Chemistry 101 as the guinea pig. I needed to get out of the hospital and back to life. Not that I didn't appreciate the efforts of the doctors or the nurses, but I have always hated hospitals.

I began my self-treatment program by making lists of random words and memorizing them backwards and forwards. Then I turned on the television and watched whatever rerun of a sixties sitcom happened to be on for fifteen minutes, shut off the aptly named boob tube and attempted to remember my list. After a few hours of self-therapy, I vainly assumed I was making excellent progress, when a stranger walked into my room expecting recognition—most likely a nurse or therapist whom I may have met during the first two days, or five minutes earlier—and my confidence was shot. This happened not once, but embarrassingly, several times. Thus progress felt painfully slow. However, by the end of the day, I was able to retain certain recent memories: the candy striper with her crisp red and white uniform who reminded me of the Swiss Miss girl, and the small army of ambulances racing to the emergency room from a very bad accident on the freeway. Little things rooted in emotional or sensory responses, but enough that I could bluff the rest. Or so I thought.

The nurses were quite cooperative in that endeavor, peppering me with questions I could easily bluff, such as: "What did you have for your last meal?"

"I had a sandwich, fruit cup, and Jello!" A bluff. I didn't remember, but that was the typical lunchtime fare at a hospital.

"That's right!"

By early evening I'd managed to convince the staff that my brain was no longer full of rudderless boats heading off into the sunset.

"Tomorrow morning will be the real test," the doctor promised. "If you can remember today tomorrow, I'll discharge." Of course I had to point out to him that if I remembered today tomorrow then what happened to yesterday? Har, har, ho, ho. He did not grasp the beauty of my sardonic wit. The joke died in a puddle on the floor, where unfortunately, a lot of my jokes meet their demise.

The first thing I did was call Sergey, my boss, to inform him I was returning to work. The weasel pretended he didn't remember me and then said they were doing just fine without me. Typical Russian humor: We don't miss you, you're nothing. Just kidding. Joke, you know, joke!

"I'm coming back tomorrow night with at least a few of my brain cells intact," I informed him. "And if you've let someone screw up Natasha's trick pony while I was gone and you expect me to fix it, I'm putting in for overtime – again!" Overtime meant money out of his budget. He'd rather pull out his fingernails than go over budget.

"Flipka, we don't let no one touch the pony again."

"Don't you Flipka me." He was lying, of course.

I hung up the phone feeling happier than I had in days. I was returning to the predictability of routine after a vacation of missed airline flights, botched hotel reservations, and bad food. Tomorrow night I pictured myself getting ready for work after a long nap and a real meal, preferably a burrito with all the trimmings at the local taco joint: overflowing with sour cream, guacamole, and a ton of hot sauce. The Russians would greet me with garlic breath, a cold shoulder, and a hard time. It was all part of the game.

What can you do for me? If nothing, what possible good are you? Look at me—I am performer, acrobat. You are lowly prop person!

Then the curtain would rise and the magic begin.

I was so wrapped in thoughts of the coming day, I didn't notice the eavesdropper standing in the door. "A few of your brain cells, hey?" he asked, an impish grin on his hobbit-like face.

"That's a few more than most people use in a lifetime. Even geniuses only use 3 percent of their brain capacity."

He walked across the room and slid into the plastic chair next to the window, letting me know with a look that I should recognize him, but I did not. He had to be someone I'd met during my hospital stay—perhaps a therapist or an administrator—but I had no idea if it was five minutes or a couple of days earlier. I'd have to bluff.

"How are you today, Fi?" he asked. "Besides anxious to get out of here."

"Do you like staying in a hospital? It's the most dangerous place on earth—full of mutated streptococci and God knows what else. Do you know 86 percent of patients leave a hospital sicker than they went in?"

"I did not."

"At any rate I'll be out of here tomorrow."

"Then what?"

"Oh I don't know. Return to life as normal."

I could tell by his face, it was the wrong answer. "Hmmm. Interesting turnabout." He quipped, looking into his hands.

I decided to try another tactic. "So what have you been up to, Sam?"

"Louie."

"Oh yeah, Louie. I'm sorry—I have this thing about names."

"No problem. I thought you'd want to know that the Nova's disappeared."

"Really?"

Why should I care if the Nova disappeared, I thought. More importantly, why did he care? Who the hell was he? A cop?

"Yes," he explained. "A woman called the wrecking yard the day after the accident and arranged to have it towed away. I think it may have been Sabrina Hyman, because the guys at the yard said she sounded like, and I quote, a 'babe'."

Apparently I'd been quite the blabbermouth. "You know, if you gave me your card the other day, I've lost it. Do you have another?"

"Not on me. Listen, you don't have much time," he said, noticing something from the window that caused him to rise up from the chair. "I'll be in touch."

"Wait a minute," I pled. What the hell was he talking about?

"Don't worry—I'll be in touch as soon as I know more."

"Merde," I swore, grabbing the nurse's button as he disappeared. What in the name of caramel candy was going on?

This stranger was followed in mere minutes by someone I wished I didn't remember.

"You hung up on me this morning, Butters!" Hyman snarled, entering my small room with a large entourage.

"They'd just given me an enema!" I lied. "I had to run to the crapper!"

That stopped him cold. It took him a few minutes, but eventually he regained his composure: "Where's my daughter, Butters?" he demanded. "Talk about crap! That story you told me was full of it!" He had all the finesse of an elephant seal on the prowl.

"You have me at a complete disadvantage, sir. Isn't Meredith with her mother?"

One eyebrow arched; a hand rose and shook menacingly, and then he grumbled, "What is this shit?" to no one in particular. "Wasn't I just here the other day, questioning that woman?"

His posse nodded in vehement agreement. Meanwhile just outside my door the third-floor nursing staff stood whispering: was that really The Doug Hyman in my room?

"Would someone please bring this man a valium?" I shouted to the nurses, "before he blows an aorta!"

"I don't need a friggin' valium, Butters. The other day, I told you about my daughter's disappearance, and in return you told me some bullshit about a mineshaft and, I don't know, some other romantic shit "

"Oh."

"Oh?"

"I don't remember—I have short-term amnesia. If you came to see me yesterday, I'm sorry, but I have no memory of the visit at all."

"What kind of excuse is that?"

"Ask one of the nurses, if they haven't all fled the building."

"Go grab a nurse, and see if her story pans out," he ordered one of his men.

"Oh Lord," I recanted, "instead of terrorizing the nursing staff, why don't you just tell me what happened—I've got at least part of my brain back now."

"The mine shaft collapsed years ago, Butters. It's impassable. You lied to me!"

"Who says?"

"The White Pine County Sheriff, that's who."

"Then how does he explain her disappearance?"

"I told you already—he thinks you have something to do with it."

"Me?"

Now Hyman wasn't a stupid man. Impatient, yes. Self-centered, yes. A bully used to getting his way, definitely. But stupid, no. I caught his eye and smirked. "Really? Does that make any logical sense?"

He turned to glare at the setting sun, causing every other living creature in the vicinity to freeze. How odd to have so much power that your quiet inspires fear in others, I thought, as I studied his Caesarian profile: hawkish nose and sunken eyes, skin reflecting the copper sunlight like an ancient Roman coin. Power and its ability to corrupt were popular debates in grad school. On one side were those who believed power was a virus so lethal that it could wipe out a person's immunity to corruption despite psychological soundness and strong moral convictions. On the other were those who believed power was only attainable through acts of corruption, some far less obvious than others. Thus, there were no so-called towers of virtue in the boardrooms or in congressional halls, only clever con men.

Of course this debate led to a research project. All debates in the psych department lead to a research project. Droning on for months as we scrambled to define our scope. (Half the battle of a research project is figuring out what you're actually researching.) Eventually it led to a very interesting conclusion having to do less with corruptibility and more with narcissism. People in positions of power fall into two categories: those with a sense of entitlement and those without. Those who felt they deserved power also felt they had papal dispensation to do whatever necessary to maintain power. On the other hand, those who felt they had been thrust into positions of power that they did not really deserve tended to be less corruptible. This is not to say they were incorruptible but they were more honestly contrite when caught with their hands in the cookie jar. I was quite sure Hyman fell into the first category. I considered asking him, if he was so worried about his daughter, why wasn't he up there himself instead of pulling everyone else around by the strings as if we were all a bunch of marionettes, but before I could muster the courage, he turned to me with a sneer.

"Butters, stop analyzing me! I feel like I'm in a damned X-ray machine."

"It is possible that not everyone is always thinking about you, you know. Maybe you're not the center of the universe. Tell me, when did Meredith disappear?"

"Yes, but you were thinking about me. I could feel it. How do you think I got to where I am?" he snarled, as one of his men desperately tried to whisper in his ear. "I got that ESP shit." Then he snarled at the man trying to get his attention, "Yes. I know what bloody time it is!"

"Did I happen to mention the idiots working down in the caves?"

"Listen, I'm not sending you up there alone this time, if that's what you mean."

Send me back there? Surely he had to be joking. "Mr. Hyman, I can't even remember what I had for breakfast, and you're sending me up to find your daughter?"

"Are you listening to me, Butters? I never repeat myself. Besides Creamo here," he said, indicating a blockish fellow with sandy-grey hair and silver mustache, "will have your back. He's a real detective—you just talk to the psycho, and you know, do your voodoo-shrink stuff. Get ready to go—you have five minutes and two days to find my daughter."

The psycho? What the hell was he talking about?

Arguing was useless. I tried and the doctor tried but to no avail. I was bundled up and hustled out of that hospital faster than a healthy newborn and shoved into a waiting block-long limo. At least the limo was equipped with a fully stocked minibar, posh seats, a pillow, a blanket, and several copies of Fly Casting Magazine, small things to be thankful for, as swearing under my breath, I contemplated my options. I could quit. Sure I could quit my job, and then he'd have no power over me, but dammit, I liked my job. Dammit, why is it that every time things seem to be going smoothly, when you finally achieve a balance and things are hunky-dory, the roof caves in? Is it the weight of some past Karma? Some reminder that you were not scheduled for the stress-free life this time? I sure as heck don't know.

"Why are we towing a Jeep?" I asked Creamo as we departed Vegas in one of those blazing pink sunsets the city is famous for.

"Mrs. Hyman needs it."

I started to chuckle, "Let me guess. Sabrina Hyman filled up the Jag with lawn mower gas and fried the engine."

He didn't respond. Creamo was a retired cop who worked for Hyman on and off—generally driving dignitaries to various casino events. He diplomatically refused comment on his employer's ex-wife. In fact, he diplomatically refused comment on any of a number of topics I tried to bring up. Finally as we headed north into the dark desert, I closed the window separating the driver's compartment so that he could smoke his Marlboros and listen to country-and-western music in peace. Poor fellow, it was a long drive. At least he was getting paid. Well, I was too, but only if you count getting to keep my job.

I figured I had three choices: I could worry all night. I could get good and pissed at Hyman. Or I could take the sleeping pill Dennis the Menace's father gave me and save my energy for whatever lay ahead. I chose the third.

CHAPTER 15

APPARENTLY WINNIE PETERSON had been very busy since I'd left, filing missing person's reports, releasing detainees, and getting her hair dyed. She'd gone from a brunette to a honey blonde. I'm no judge of feminine beauty but from the expression on Creamo's face, it wasn't a bad move on her part.

"You mean Meredith just walked out of here by herself after dark?" I asked, as we gagged down reheated coffee in her office. I'd slept until almost nine, thanks to the miracle of modern medicine, awakening to a persistent rapping on the window of the limo. It was Creamo. He'd already poked around Enev, asking questions and making notes in his steno pad, and now he was ready for coffee. Luckily my morning grooming routine was brief.

"At first we thought she left with you . . ." Ms. Peterson asserted.

I couldn't reply in any way that was not insulting, so I kept my mouth shut.

She got the point. "But once we heard about your accident . . ." She paused to fluff her hair with freshly manicured fingers. "We assumed that some boy was waiting for her outside the gate and that in all the excitement that night, she managed to slip past the guard. Meredith Hyman was getting letters from several young men—did you know that?"

Was this the same Winnie Peterson that I met last week, I thought, dressed in stylish tweed trousers and tan cashmere pullover. The picture of the man in the wheelchair was missing from behind her desk; lying in its place was a set of keys on a Mercedes key chain.

"It doesn't surprise me that she would have a ton of boyfriends," I admitted, "but if that was her plan, one of the other girls might know something that could help us locate her. Can we at least talk to the others?"

"You can talk to Nancy Jean—she's still in detention. Leticia and Bonny have both been released via our early release program for first-time offenders."

"What?"

"They were scheduled for release in the next six months, and we needed their beds. Budget cuts, you know. Leticia was released to her grandfather, and I'm sorry, but I don't have an address for him. We referred Bonny to an independent-living-skills program down in Vegas. She was close enough to emancipation that . . ."

"She was sixteen, wasn't she?"

"Yeah, but what were they going to do with her? A group home? How long do you think that would have lasted?"

"And the little Vietnamese girl?"

"After Meredith left, she tried to hurt herself. We had to transfer her to White Pine Hospital down in Caliente."

Mighty convenient, I thought to myself. Two girls released and one in a psych ward fifty miles away. The only one left, locked in detention and probably heavily sedated. I turned to Creamo, but he had no expression on his face as he jotted notes on his steno pad. I must admit, having him along made dealing with Ms. Peterson a piece of cake. Something about his aura of big-city cop so clearly trumped her tough prison matron that she was working on a whole new shtick, one designed to make her appear cooperative and reasonable. Creamo maintained a solid cool, responding not in the least when she insisted on walking us up to the cemetery in the freezing drizzle to show us that the mine shaft had been blocked by a cave-in "some years before."

"Looks fresh," he whispered to me. Of course it was fresh! There hadn't even been an attempt to cover up the deep, muddy ruts left by dump trucks! It was so obviously a lie that it made my blood boil, but instead I followed Creamo's lead.

After this ridiculous lie, Ms. Peterson allowed us to interview several staff members and the guard on duty, review the visitor's log, and confiscate any of Meredith Hyman's possessions that her mother had not taken, including letters from her many beaux. Creamo examined the girl's various trinkets gingerly—love beads and peace symbols, postcards from friends, paperbacks, and lip glosses—as though each was a special treasure. Watching him I realized he'd probably watched her grow up and developed a familial affection for her. Or perhaps, I postulated further, he had a daughter of his own, rebellious and whimsical, who'd captivated him and then, through a marital breakup (he wore no wedding ring) had disappeared.

"Where's her diary?" I asked Ms. Peterson.

"How do you know she kept a diary?"

"Don't most teenaged girls? I remember my first diary was hardly bigger than a wallet. I was so afraid I'd lose the key, that I wore it around my neck on a chain."

"Not all teenaged girls keep diaries these days!" Ms. Peterson supplied, as though I'd been born in Victorian times. "But if she did have one, her mother now has it." She paused before concluding, "is that all? Because I'm due in court in Elko this afternoon."

"Do you know where Mrs. Hyman went after you discovered her daughter was missing?"

"I presume the hotel in Ely."

Peterson had given us an hour. It was now up. She walked us to the limo expecting us to leave, but instead I reminded her that we needed to talk to Nancy Jean. "It'll do you no good," she stated. I insisted, and so she ordered her second-in-command to escort us to detention. The woman mumbled that she had better things to do, there being a flu epidemic in half the barracks and Ms. Peterson out for the rest of the day. But she changed her tune when Creamo rubbed his thumb and middle finger together: the universal sign that cooperation would be rewarded.

The detention barracks reminded me of an animal shelter. It was the smell. Girls who broke the rules at Enev were not allowed any of the usual perfumery that the other girls so lavishly doused themselves in, and thus, the place reeked of ammonia. Each girl in solitary was assigned a closetlike room in which there was a sink, a cot, and a chair. The bathrooms were at the end of the hall. To use them, girls had to call upon the on-duty matron and be escorted down the hall. This rarely happened. The girls merely used their sinks as toilets. Where the hell were the goddamn state inspectors, I thought. We weren't in Morocco or Thailand—this was the USA.

Even without her Cleopatra eye makeup, I had to remind myself that Nancy Jean was only sixteen years old. Her eyes had no shine, her hair no natural luster. She'd been scraped clean of hope. "It's colder than hell in here," she complained as I sat on the plastic chair. "Can you tell them to turn up the heat?"

"Why don't I see if I can get you out of here? You were only supposed to be in here for the weekend."

"They'll never let me out."

According to her chart, they'd put her on mood-altering drugs for a grossly premature diagnosis of schizophrenia. I'd seen it happen before. Slap on a preliminary diagnosis of bipolar, depression, or schizophrenia, and you could get a prescription of any number of mood-altering drugs strong enough to turn the most hard-core badass into a zombie. Take the fight out of the little stinkers instead of dealing with their loss of self-esteem and hope.

"They hate me. Can you at least get me a ciggie?"

"Can I get you a cigarette? I'm a doctor—what kind of question is that?"

"I'm going to die young anyway—so who cares."

"Mr. Creamo—do you mind parting with one of your Marlboros?"

Creamo nodded, handing her a cigarette, and then backed off, as if she might bite.

"Now, I can't let you light it in here," I explained, handing her the cancer stick. Her fingers were stained, fingernails bitten back into the flesh. "But you can put it in your mouth and pretend."

"What good will that do?"

"Oral gratification. It's my best offer. Now talk—where did that mine tunnel lead to?"

"Does he have to be here?"

"Don't worry about him. He's my driver."

"No he's not. He's a cop and why do you call him Creamo?"

"I don't know. Let's ask him."

Creamo took in a deep breath and mumbled. "Hyman thinks I take too much cream in my coffee. Thinks it's gonna kill me someday."

"That's the stupidest thing I've ever heard," she cackled. "Just stupid."

"Well then you can call me Detective Bahnhof, young lady."

"Detective Train Station! That's even stupider. You guys are so stupid! A lot of girls have disappeared, but of course, when Meredith Hyman disappears, it's a big deal. The rest of us are just trash, so who cares!"

"Listen, kid. I'll see what I can do to get you out of here, but you gotta tell us what you know."

"I was locked in detention! I don't know anything about goddamn Meredith Hyman!"

"Yeah, but before you were locked up in here, tell us where you and the other girls went. Where does the mine tunnel lead to?"

"What mine tunnel? I don't know what the hell you're talking about."

"Let's go." I said to Creamo. "Sorry I wasted your time with Miss Terminal Wiseass here."

We were halfway out the front door when she screamed, "Wait!"

CHAPTER 16

AS SOON AS WE WERE OUT of sight, Creamo stopped the limo by the side of the road. "Tell me," he asked, as we got out to unhitch the Jeep, "what was she in for?"

"Nothing much—just a little murder and mayhem," I chuckled, rapping on the window of the passenger compartment. "You can come out now, Nancy Jean. Time for show-and-tell."

"Should I cuff her?" he asked, as she sheepishly crept into the sunlight, her scrawny body looking even more pathetic in one of my bulky sweatshirts. Luckily, the state doesn't pay well. A wad of Hyman's cash to the matron in charge, and she was ours for an hour, hopefully to keep her promise.

"No, don't cuff her," I replied stupidly. "What harm can she do?"

"Remember your promise," she whined, the soggy cigarette still dangling from her lip.

"Could you give her a light please, Creamo?"

"You're the doc."

I didn't feel like much of a doctor, watching a sixteen-year-old puff away. Damn Hyman for putting me in this position; damn Meredith Hyman for disappearing; damn the cavalry for coming out to fight the Indians. Damn them all!

Taking the Jeep, we drove to the ridge behind Enev, from where we could see the other less significant mountains in Cavalry Peak's shadow. The area was rarely explored, as it had nothing of significance to offer either hunters or adventure junkies, no hunting lodges or pristine lakes, just struggling bristle cones and scrubby hills. Following the girl's direction, we drove down the rocky slope to a narrow gulch bordered on either side by distinctive rock formations so symmetrical that they resembled manufactured steel beams leaning against the side of the building. I'd seen similar rock formations in the high Sierra, called Devil's Post Pile or Satan's Furnace, but such formations of basalt were rare (or so I thought) in an area so relatively low in altitude. I was about to point out this geological oddity when Creamo began his interrogation of our prisoner:

"Where is it, young lady?"

"We have to find the Space Man," Nancy Jean replied, as she puffed away in the back seat.

"What is the Space Man?" I asked.

"The Space Man points to the caves of Osceola. That's where you'll find Merry."

Creamo slammed on the brakes. At first I thought his disgust with Nancy Jean had percolated from simmer to boil, but actually it was a series of fresh tire treads crisscrossing our path that caused him to stop. "These ruts are fresh," he said. "I bet this is where she met the fella. Yeah, I bet she got through one of those breaches in the back fence—cripes, did you see that thing? Goddamn worst security I've ever seen. Yup, out the back fence, over the hill, and there he was, waiting."

"That's not true!" Nancy Jean interrupted. "She hated all her old boyfriends!"

"Yeah, why have a flesh-and-blood boyfriend when she could have a dead one?" Creamo laughed. He'd barely endured, the (to him) bullshit story that Meredith Hyman was infatuated with a ghost. All dames, young or old, lived to torment men. Real men, not ghosts. He continued, "If I can get some good shots of these prints and send them to the lab, they should be able to tell us what make of vehicle we're looking for. Yup, should be able to wrap this thing up pretty quick now."

"That's not true—she was going to find Echoing waters."

"Oh Lord," Creamo groaned, glaring over the seat at Nancy Jean. "Not this horse crap again. Just tell us the name of the idiot she's with."

She began to tremble, "I need another ciggie."

Creamo tapped his fingers on the steering wheel. "We're wasting our time with this little piece of shit. I don't know why I let you talk me into it. I feel sorry for your parents, you little dipshit."

"You're an asshole!" Nancy Jean screamed, shutting down like a windup toy whose spring had sprung.

"I thought I was supposed to handle this," I whispered. "Isn't that why Hyman insisted I accompany you? This kid's heard it all before. That she's not worthy of attention, affection, or even love from a too-busy mother and absent father. Probably heard it from the moment she was born and, by dint of too much hair or common facial features, immediately became the apple that had fallen too far from the tree, the child neither side wanted to claim, the freckle in the cradle of the unblemished."

"Save the bleeding-heart bullshit. She's bluffing. She doesn't know nothing."

I'd considered that possibility. That her tough act was a ruse to get attention, any attention—even negative attention. She was definitely smart enough to yank our chains. Part of me didn't blame her, but I didn't have time to deal with her wide variety of psychoses through the normal channels. Meredith Hyman was missing, and until she was found, I was screwed.

"Hey I have an idea," I whispered to Creamo.

"Yeah?"

"Not here—lock her in the car, and come away from it for a minute. I need to talk to you in private." He was leery, but he did as I asked. As we stood shivering on the ridge, I told him my plan. He gave exactly the response I expected to hear.

"Hypnotism? It's a sham! I've seen police use it, and it never works."

"It's a myth," I explained, "that people will do something under hypnosis they wouldn't do if fully conscious, like confess to murder. Especially if said murderer is a sociopath."

"Exactly—if she won't tell us anything now, why will she under hypnosis?"

"Because I plan to tap into her memory through regression. Remember the therapist who regressed a Colorado housewife back to another lifetime—the Bridey Murphy case? Folks got all excited, until it turned out she was remembering stories told to her by a neighbor when she was three! Regression was pooh-poohed for a time as unacceptable therapy, even quackery, but I think . . ."

"Oh, for the love of Pete!" Creamo groaned. He was looking past me to the car. "What the hell is she doing now?"

Nancy Jean had removed all of her clothes and was now slithering over the backseat and onto the front like a slippery, pink eel in a black fright wig. She nestled behind the steering wheel and began frantically seesawing the wheel like a four-year-old on a joyride.

"Should have cuffed her," Creamo snarled.

I had to agree he was right. "Look at it this way," I explained, "our only clue to what happened to Meredith is a psychotic teenager. If she knows anything at all, if there is any island of sanity in her mind, we need to get through to it. Think of hypnotism as our boat."

He watched in disgust, as Nancy Jean licked the dashboard and then, realizing she'd scored an audience, smashed her naked breasts against the window. They looked like two eggs over easy. "Come and get me," she howled.

Alas, I had no valium or I would have given one to Creamo and taken one myself.

"Ok, Doc," he sighed. "I'll get some pictures of the tire treads, while you go fishing in the psycho's noggin."

CHAPTER 17

BY THE TIME we finally got to Ely, the coffee shop at the Old Ely Hotel and Gambling Hall had quit serving lunch, and the waitress, who'd been working since four thirty am, had no sympathy for us. We could walk across the street to the Dairy Queen. Or get munchies in the hotel bar. Or drive down the street to the market and make our own damn sandwiches for all she cared. Her coffee shop was closed. We had a two-thirty appointment with the sheriff, which didn't leave a lot of time to find a bite to eat so Creamo opted for the bar (the Dairy Queen didn't serve whiskey). Besides he couldn't leave the hotel; Doug Hyman would be calling momentarily for an update.

"I need a bit more than peanuts and pretzels. I'm going across the street to the DQ. Want something?" I asked.

"What if Hyman calls?"

"What if?"

"No," Creamo ordered, "you better stay here. Someone has to tell him why we just wasted a grand on that little dipshit and it's not going to be me. You know, this isn't one of those detective shows where the rich guy hands you a wad of cash to get a job done and doesn't care how you spend it. Hyman cares. Trust me, he cares where every penny . . ."

"Just tell him that . . ."

"No, no, no. You tell him! It's your wacky theory. You know what I think."

Creamo wasn't buying the notion that Meredith Hyman had gone in search of an underground Shangri-La described in the journal of a long-dead cavalryman. He'd already ordered someone in Las Vegas to track down her past-and-present boyfriends, and now it was just a matter of time before one of those acne-ridden, lovesick hounds confessed. Then he would pick up Merry and rough up the boyfriend. Case solved.

"I thought Sabrina Hyman was staying at this hotel," I asked, as I followed him into the abandoned bar. "Shouldn't we talk to her too? After all, she was there the night—"

Creamo ignored me. "Bartender!" he yelled. Behind the heavily shellacked bar sat row upon row of tempting libations but, alas, no bartender to serve them.

"I can't imagine what it must have been like for her—by herself out here with her daughter missing. I think I would have gone crazy," I continued.

"Bartender!" he yelled again. Until he got relief, I'd have better luck stirring up a conversation with a slot machine.

Like the hotel itself, the "saloon" (as it liked to be called) had resisted all attempts at modernization, except for the addition of electronic gambling devices and pinball machines ching-ching-chinging in every nook and cranny, even on a still-as-death afternoon in October. It was the same all over Nevada, gambling machines and pinball machines in restaurants, grocery stores, laundromats—all businesses save funeral homes. And, then it was probably only a matter of time before an enterprising mortician broke through that particular barrier of decency and installed a slot machine in his waiting room. Ho! Or, maybe he would decide to create the first drive-through funeral home. Drive up. View the departed. Drive away. Next!

"Where is the goddamn bartender?" Creamo scowled, after a few minutes of playing piano with his knuckles.

"The bartender is probably in the back doing the lunchtime dishes," I chuckled. "It's not exactly the height of tourist season. Why not help yourself? And while you're at it, hand me some pretzels."

I couldn't blame Creamo for being grouchy. Thanks to me, he was low on cigarettes and even lower on patience. We'd had to bribe Nancy Jean with his Marlboros to get her to put her clothes back on. (I have a strict policy against hypnotizing naked people.) Then he'd had to occupy himself in the cold, snapping photos of tire treads while he waited.

I'd used Braid's technique to put the girl under. It's the oldest and most ridiculed method, cartoonish in its simplicity but remarkably successful. "Nancy Jean, focus on the silver dollar," I'd ordered.

"You can't hypnotize me!"

"Oh yeah."

I swung my silver dollar key chain back and forth about a foot from her face. "You're not going under. You're just feeling sleepy." I have to admit I felt a little silly, sitting in a Jeep in the middle of the desert in broad daylight, trying to put a girl under. Luckily, she proved to be extraordinarily susceptible to suggestion, following the silver dollar with her eyes until her lids drooped close. I must admit, I was surprised. Susceptibility to hypnotism generally correlates to open-mindedness. Not a trait generally associated with surly teenage girls.

"Nancy Jean, I want you to return to the day when you girls first found the mine."

Her chin slumped down to her chest, a sign that she was regressing, and then she muttered without expression, "We didn't find it. Merry did. She was always wandering around the cemetery making up romantic shit about the dead people. It's so stupid."

"Where did she find the journal?"

"In the tunnel. Stupid."

For a second I was afraid I'd lost her, or that she was pretending. Her eyes fluttered beneath closed lids. Her shoulders crimped. "Oh, how stupid," she finally muttered. "I'm not going."

"Where? Where aren't you going?"

"Merry wants us to come with her into the tunnel. I'm not going! Lettie says that cannibals live in the mountain. They ate the miner's children. Stole them in the middle of the night, slaughtered them like baby pigs and then cooked their bodies over the fire. Merry says that's stupid. She has a flashlight she stole from Palmer House, and she's going down into the mine whether we're going or not."

She began twitching again. "Nancy Jean, what's happening now."

"There's a strange light ahead. This is weird, really weird. Something . . ."

"Nancy Jean, where are you now?"

"At the pool."

"The pool?"

"The tunnel ends at the pool. It's like the ground caved in—I see sunlight above, and below is a pool of green water that kind of glows like a swimming pool at night, you know, one of those in-ground pools that has underwater lamps. My mother's always trying to get Dad to buy one for her but he won't. She's says she needs it for her arthritis, but she just wants to have her friends over for one of her dumb parties. Wait for me, Lettie, wait for me."

"What's happening?"

"Merry's found a box—a metal box lying there like it was waiting for her or something."

She was quiet again.

"Nancy Jean?"

"It had the book. Seb's book and the ointment. What's that noise? Is someone coming?"

"Nancy Jean?"

"That's all. We left. But the book, the book said Echoing waters was just beyond the pool . . ."

That was as far as I got before Creamo ran out of pictures to take—and patience. He opened the front door. "We're out of here," he announced, shaking the blowing sand from his hair like a wet dog. The girl quickly snapped out of the trance, leaving me more confused than ever. She described a cenote, a sink hole like those you'd find in the jungles of the Yucatan, not the parched deserts of Nevada. Had I just walked her back to a childhood memory?

Luckily the bartender turned out to be a young lady with a good sense of humor and an ever-so-much-nicer personality than the waitress at the coffee shop who I found out, after an unfortunate comment, happened to be her mother. Insult to mother aside, she rustled up leftovers of that day's meatloaf special from the kitchen. Creamo wouldn't eat it. He had stomach ulcers that apparently were unfazed by Jack Daniels. He sat at the bar trying to ignore me. Then he went to his room to make a few calls, while I snuck across the street for an ice cream cone.

The sheriff, almost an hour late, readily accepted Creamo's offer of a Coors draft and then wrapped himself awkwardly across from us in a corner booth in the bar. He was a long, lean man with a nervous tick and a cowboy hat twice as big as it needed to be.

"We think Meredith Hyman was picked up by a boyfriend outside the reformatory last Saturday night," Creamo explained.

"That's exactly what I said."

"Have you canvassed the local hotels?"

"Why would I want to do that?"

"To find out if any strangers had checked in recently."

"Who else would check into a hotel in these areas but a stranger?"

Creamo changed gears: "According to your report, the matron in charge of the barracks said she saw Meredith Hyman at lights out—9 pm—and yet an hour later when Miss Peterson and her mother went to get her, she was gone. Did you speak to the matron directly?"

"Of course. Why would you ask that?"

"Because in the report you refer to the woman as, and I quote, 'Miss Smith.' The matron for Meredith Hyman's barracks is named Isabella Rodriquez."

The sheriff huffed up like a rooster: "You gotta understand, a lot of people go missing out here so when some privileged brat disappears from Enev, I'm not gonna screw up my Sunday over it—and I don't care who her daddy is. He can come up here and kiss my ass!"

The sheriff spoke loudly enough for any nearby voter to hear and then, noting Creamo's reaction, softened his tone: "Look, Enev is on federal land and it's a state facility. We generally don't get involved in their affairs. I mean, if an inmate escapes from any other prison, the sheriff doesn't file a missing person's report, now does he?"

"Then why did you take the report?"

"Because Sabrina Hyman insisted. She said technically her daughter was no longer a detainee and that she had reason to believe she was hiding some place on Enev—some mine tunnel or cave or something. She wanted me to arrange a search party. So I went out there with her the next morning and looked around. She's a real looker, you know. Classy but not too, you know, hoity-toity. But the mine tunnel had caved in years ago, according to Peterson, so there was no way the girl could be down there."

"When did, ah, Sabrina Hyman arrive in town?"

The sheriff chuckled, "Late Saturday night. It was hard to miss her!"

"What do you mean?"

"The engine of that foreign pile of crap of hers blew up right in front of the station, and then she went wacko, I tell you! She wouldn't calm down till I promised to give old Winnie Ralston a visit."

"Winnie Ralston?"

"Did I say Ralston? Well, I meant Winnie Peterson."

Creamo, who wrote down everything in his steno pad, boldly underlined Ralston. "I see. How long have you known Ms. Peterson?"

"Well, she's been out at Enev a dozen or so years but no one knows too much about her. I only see her when she comes into Ely for a hearing at the courthouse, and then she's gone; she doesn't hang around and have dinner or nothing."

"You mean you didn't take a missing person's when the counselor disappeared? I have . . ."

"Oh, that. Oh yeah. Well, her parents came to town, you see, claimed she'd never go anywhere without her Bible. Some folks are real clueless about their kids, know what I mean?"

"Where is Mrs. Hyman now?"

"I haven't seen her since Sunday afternoon, but I heard she's out at Longleys."

"What's that?"

The Sheriff chuckled. "It's a cathouse! A high-class cathouse, but a cathouse nonetheless. The lady who owns the place, Sal Longley, used to be Vegas showgirl before she inherited the ranch. I guess that's how them two ladies hooked up in the first place."

"Figures," Creamo moaned, "I know Sal Longley."

"You know, they had to tow Sabrina's foreign piece of shit all the way to Elko. No mechanic in this neck of the woods would even touch it."

"Did you talk to the other girls in Meredith's barracks?" I asked. "Bonny, Thanh or Leticia?"

"Shit, Dr. Butters. You ever talk to those girls out at that place?"

"Did you know they're no longer out at Enev? According to Ms. Peterson, two were released and the third was supposedly sent to the psychiatric facility in Pioche? Convenient, don't you think?"

"Like I said, that's a state facility. None of our business."

CHAPTER 18

CREAMO FELL ASLEEP listening to me explain how Rheobatrachus vitellinus, a gastric breeder (unfortunately now extinct), held far more promise for healing what ailed him (in my humble opinion) than genus Epipedobates tricolor, or as Creamo called them, the poison frogs.

"Rheobatrachus had the ability to shut down their gastric juices during gestation, which occurred inside their stomachs. Think about what that would mean for people suffering from ulcers!" I explained as we waited in the bar for Hyman's checkup call.

He yawned. Lack of sleep, two whiskeys, and a beer had slowed him to a crawl. "You want me to raise frogs in my stomach? What kind of a doctor were you?"

"Don't be silly," I laughed. "My point is long-term studies done on other species of amphibians have led researchers to theorize that, aside from producing a pain killer, epibatidine—which is two hundred times as potent as morphine—secretions from, say, Phyllobates terribilis (the Golden Poison Frog) are not beneficial in treating gastrointestinal disorders, despite what you may have heard. Secretions from dendrobatids are showing promise as muscle relaxants and heart stimulants, but there have been, instead of improvements, serious gastronomical side effects, and so I would highly recommend that you steer clear of any doctor wanting to sign you up for a clinical trial involving Phyllobates terribilis. I would instead look into—"

Creamo's eyelids drooped shut.

"—biofeedback techniques for stress which have shown some success in treating ulcers; however . . ."

His head slid against the side of the booth as both shoulders slumped and arms fell limp. He was out for the count, bored into slumber by yours truly. The bar, on the other hand, was beginning to show signs of life. There were the obvious "regulars" flirting with the bartender, a scene that (from the expression on her face) played out night after night, a smattering of young cowboys hunched around the jukebox, yakking about the day's events, and a group of seniors waiting for the coffee shop to open for the four-dollar-and-fifty-cent early-bird special.

I found it odd that Creamo had no interest in talking to Sabrina Hyman, especially after the Sheriff proved to be so worthless. Despite what he thought of her, she had arranged for her daughter's release and had driven all the way from Lake Tahoe to bring her home. Not to mention the fact that she was there the night Meredith disappeared. I decided to take matters into my own hands.

"How do I get out to a place called Longley Ranch?" I asked the bartender after I managed to get her attention by rudely inserting myself into the throng of her admirers.

"Longley's?" She replied. "You don't want to go out to Longley's!"

"Why not? I was thinking of applying for a job."

This statement elicited a froglike croak from the man at my elbow. I turned to him: "I guess I'm not your type, hey?" He mumbled something under his breath, picked up his beer, and moved as far away from me as he could and still be seated at the bar. I turned to the bartender. "Seriously, I need to talk to someone I think might be out there."

"Well," she began, "there's a man in town who drives customers out there, waits for them, and then brings them back into town."

"Oh, you can just tell me where it is; I'll just drive out there."

"You'll never find it. Besides, they shoot before they ask questions. Their higher-end customers arrive by private plane and take a copter from the airstrip to the ranch."

"That sounds pretty fancy-schmanzy."

"You've got that right."

"Could you put me in touch with the pimp?"

"He only takes customers; he won't take policemen."

"The cop's asleep. We've had a rough day. When and if he does wake up, tell him I should be back by dark. Don't tell him I went out to the cathouse unless, of course, I never return."

She hesitated.

"I'm a shrink. I've worked with prostitutes before."

She made the call.

There are hundreds of brothels in Nevada. Some are legal; most are not. If you ask most "working gals", they'd rather work for an illegal operation where they're not licensed, taxed, and tracked by law enforcement, poked and prodded by condescending health workers, and abused by managers who are little more than slave owners. Legal brothels advertise freely, even putting signs on the highway, promising all sorts of extras like all night parking for truckers. Dirt is cheap on the edge of nowhere. The illegal ones are only known by word of mouth. While I was not an expert on brothels, I strongly suspected that Longley Ranch would not have a sign or a parking lot the size of a football field, and I was right. It was about fifteen minutes outside of town, down an unmarked exit off the highway, over a couple of white-rocked ridges, and into a spring-fed valley at the bottom of a mountain range that looked like a pile of rocks. There were several structures, all sharing a relatively level plot next to a struggling stream: a three-story Cape Cod in good repair, a shabby barn, and a long, narrow, aluminum-sided building that didn't belong in the scene at all. Although it doesn't sound like much, it was mighty posh for an unlicensed cathouse over four hours from Vegas.

"You have a half hour, and then I'm heading back to town," the taxi driver informed me. I paid him (it was a cash-in-advance proposition) and then started walking down the path toward the house. I didn't get too far. I was stopped in my tracks by the bouncer or whatever they call the man who deals with difficult customers at a brothel.

"Regular customers go there," he snarled—pointing to the aluminum building.

"I'm not a customer—I'm here to talk to Sabrina Hyman."

"No hablo Ingles."

No hablo Ingles my ass, I thought. "Well, can I talk to someone who does?"

"Customers—there," he reiterated. He wasn't that large a man but something told me he didn't need to be. Maybe it was the scars on his well-tanned face or the way he held his right hand floating above his waist at hip level, like a gunfighter. I decided to try my luck with the woman standing in the door of the building I was directed to. She didn't look like an ex-showgirl. She looked like an ex–Roller Derby queen.

"Are you Sal Longley?" I asked.

"Nope, I ain't," she replied as she led me inside. "Listen, I think we have just the girl for you; but you never know. Give 'em all a look and let me know."

"Ah, no. You don't understand."

"I got nothing against your type," she said, dragging me into the building. "Long as you have money, course. Cash."

Oh, Lord. Inside the building, five females stood against the wall in lingerie. None of them looked me in the eye.

"I'm not a customer," I reiterated. "I'm looking for Sabrina Hyman—she's the ex-wife of Doug Hyman. You know—Mr. Las Vegas?"

The madam thought for a moment. "You'll still have to pay," she explained. "You think the driver brings people out here for free? He'll expect a cut."

"I already paid him."

"Huh, doesn't matter. Thirty dollars."

"OK,OK. Can you at least tell me if she's here?"

"Who wants to know?"

"Fi Butters. Doctor Fi Butters."

"I'll check up at the house," she said, taking my money. A twenty and a ten.

"Can I have a receipt for my expense report?" I asked.

"You're kidding," she chuckled. "Back to your rooms, girls. No sale."

As they trod back toward their rooms, it was hard to tell whether they were relieved or disappointed at not having a customer. None were very pretty; a few looked decidedly underage, which surprised me. Brothels run by women are generally more careful. Don't ask me why. Maybe it's because the women are in it for the money. Getting caught pimping an underage girl results in a hefty fine. Not good business. Male brothel owners, on the other hand, get their jollies breaking in the young girls, thus they're more willing to take the chance.

One of the girls glanced up from her feet as she passed. Her eyes were blank; her complexion shallow. It was as if the skin on her face had been stretched over plump flesh by a taxidermist. I'd seen that look before.

"Leticia?" I asked.

She looked me in the eye. No, it wasn't her. The eyes were wrong— close, but wrong. A light shade of grey instead of pale blue. "Do you know someone named Leticia Honeywell, because you look just like her?"

"She's my sister."

"You want to talk to this woman?" the madam intervened.

"Yes. I'm trying to find a girl who was released from Enev a couple of days ago."

"We don't take the girls from Enev—they're damaged goods, too hard to control. You might want to check out Dolly Lama's. They take 'em."

"Look, I just want to ask this young lady a few questions."

"If you want to talk to this woman, it'll be fifty."

"Why?"

"Because homosexuality is a sin."

Shit, I thought, it's because she's underage and you know it, Lady. But I kept my big mouth shut.

Leticia's sister claimed to be eighteen (the legal age for prostitution in Nevada), but she was lying. She chewed gum with her mouth open as though faulty adenoids had left her with a breathing problem. She had a child's hands and, though thin, still maintained a telltale roll of baby fat around her waist. I judged her to be no older than fourteen, as I perched on the edge of her twin-sized bed, cringing at the thought of what went on in the crinkled sheets just inches from my fingers.

"Do you know that your sister was recently released from the reformatory?" I asked.

"No," she replied.

"Do you know where I can find your grandfather?"

"No. I haven't seen him for a long time."

She focused on a row of silver bracelets dangling from her wrist as she mumbled. They sounded like wind chimes tinkling in the breeze, probably a soothing sound to focus on while being treated like a piece of property. Not only did she look underage, but she was dressed like a preteen at a slumber party, in a skintight Mickey Mouse tee shirt and flannel hot pants. I gagged down a sudden hatred for men.

"Where do you live? They can't keep you here all the time."

"Ha!" she mumbled.

"They don't let you go home?"

"I don't have a home. They have a place up in Elko where we can go when we're off. It's a real house with a pool, and as long as we're working here, we can go up there for a break, you know, and then we can go to the movies or the mall as long as we're not working solo—that would be real bad; that's how girls get hurt. I wouldn't do that, you know, 'cause they take good care of us . . ."

"Wait—you don't have to defend this place. I'm not an inspector, really. I'm not even a detective. I'm just a lady who's trying to find your sister. Have you been in touch with her?"

"Nope. She doesn't know where I am; she probably thinks I'm still in Reno. That's where we were when she got busted. But she wouldn't go stay with Grandpa Fergie. He's a nutcase."

"Nutcases are my specialty. What happened to your parents?"

"I don't have a dad. My mom ran off and left us with Grandpa Fergie when I was in kindergarten. He told everybody that the Indians in Cavalry Peak got her and they ate her alive. He's obsessed with that mountain. We never had any friends 'cause of the cats."

"The cats?"

"Yup. He likes to stuff them. Creeps people out."

Grandpa Fergie started to sound real familiar.

"Did you run away from him? Is that how you ended up here?"

"No. One day the police showed up with this smiley-faced lady. There was blood all over the floor. Grandpa'd just shot a couple cats and one of them was split open on the kitchen table. The policeman gave us a couple of black plastic bags, like the kind you use for garbage and told us to throw all our stuff in the bags and go with Smiley Face. I don't know what they did with Grandpa Fergie—I didn't care. First they took us to this place where a nurse shaved off all our hair and then scrubbed our bodies down with some awful-smelling soap. They said we had lice. Then they took us to Miss Jean's. That was an awful place. We had to scrub the floors with bleach every day, or else we couldn't watch TV. The smiley-faced woman came by every now and then, and Miss Jean would lie to her about us and say really bad things. Finally they split us up. The smiley-faced lady split us up—I hated her after that. Even when she came up all nicey-nicey I wouldn't talk to her. When Lettie got old enough, she ran away and came and got me. I guess you can kind of figure out the rest of the story. Anyway, I don't want to talk about it anymore."

Suddenly the madam knocked on the door, ordering me to follow her to the Cape Cod. I wanted to give the girl a big hug and tell her that everything would be okay, but I stopped myself. She'd already been told too many lies by smiley-faced ladies.

The Cape Cod was for "special" customers, presumably those who came via private jet and helicopter. The ground floor looked like an advertisement in Home and Garden's southwest edition: plaid sofas, Indian pottery and Remington prints on the wall. The woman who introduced herself at the front door as Sal Longley was petite, well preserved, and over bronzed, holding what appeared to be a martini, dirty, on the rocks, with three olives. She informed me in a businesslike manner that Sabrina Hyman could be found in the sunroom "twirling."

"I'd like to have a few words alone with you, Doctor Butters."

Gads, I thought, I'm busted. I'll never get out of here alive. She knows that as a psychiatrist, I'm required by law to report all forms of child abuse, such as employing underage prostitutes. Hopefully she's just going to threaten me (beware dark alleys and deserted streets) and not something worse.

I was wrong. She wanted to tell me her theory on Meredith Hyman's disappearance, and it was a doozy.

Conspiracy theories always find fertile ground in Nevada. They're like tumbleweeds. They don't need solid roots. They travel fast and suck the air out of the countryside. They clog the engines of functioning vehicles. They collect and mount higher and higher, blocking any way out. Some are just laughable; others can have serious repercussions such as the Hippie Panic of the late sixties when law enforcement officials, egged on by local units of the John Birch Society, became convinced longhairs from nearby California planned to move in and take over the state, turning it into a haven for the unwashed and over hairy. Some moron running for office even suggested that they (the hippies) had already moved in and were mingling sinisterly with the local, innocent population. Sort of a hippie version of Invasion of the Body Snatchers. Soon LSD would be legalized. There would be orgies in the streets! Anarchy! Chaos! The mass hysteria generated by this idiot spread from small cities to redneck grottos far and wide across the state. In no time, if you were pulled over for a speeding ticket in Winnemucca, Nevada, you'd have a better chance of making it out of that town alive if you were black than if you looked like a hippie.

I listened to Sal Longley's conspiracy story with a straight face, almost wishing I had a glass of whatever she was drinking. Then I tried to inject a bit of sanity. "Winnie Peterson is about as warm and fuzzy as a barracuda, but I'm sure she's not selling unwanted girls to some . . . what did you call it? An international sex trafficking outfit?"

"That broad just turns her back when they disappear. Besides, I have proof."

"What's that?"

"They've thrown back some of the girls they didn't want. Like garbage—it's disgusting."

"Oh." Goody, I thought, a morality lesson from a woman who pimps underage girls.

"Yeah they're only taking the good stuff."

"Well," I sighed, "I gotta tell you, it's not like Enev is full of beautiful fresh young things—half of them belong in mental institutions."

"You'll see when the truth comes out."

The woman was suffering from alcohol-induced dementia. "I'm sure I will. Say, the taxi driver only gave me a half hour. Suppose I can talk to Sabrina?"

She directed me to the back of the house and then disappeared upstairs. An odd woman, I thought. Not really evil so much as completely devoid of warmth, merely a business woman complaining about an unfair competitive advantage. She didn't care that girls might be sold into slavery, only about the effect the practice would have on her bottom line.

In the middle of a sparsely furnished sunroom, Sabrina Hyman twirled in long white robes, her blonde hair tied back into a ponytail. She saw me but did not stop.

"What going on? This place is empty." I joked as she tried to explain the importance of whirling to maintain a sense of equilibrium. It was some Sufi belief. Twirl till the resulting dizziness puts you in line with the universe. Twirl till you forget that you've misplaced the bookmark and must begin again on the first page. Twirl, twirl, twirl.

"Oh, you mean the customers? Sal gets most of her business Mondays and Fridays, businessmen traveling back and forth from Salt Lake to California in their private jets. I think she was smart to buy this place, don't you? Although I think she inherited it. I can't remember."

"Could you stop spinning? I'm getting dizzy."

"Really? You could have never been a dancer," she giggled. "We have to twirl and twirl and twirl." She floated into a beanbag on the floor, her robes billowing around her like a sea of marshmallow fluff. "I think this place is much better than the others, because the girls don't have to stand around—the clients get these videotape thingies, and then, you know, they pick the one they want, and so when they get here, the girl is waiting for them in their own separate suite. Cool, huh?" she asked.

"I've always longed to know the modern marvels of a first-rate cathouse," I chuckled, but my attempt at irony fell flat. She just looked up at me confused. What a huge waste of time, I thought, she probably doesn't even know what day it is.

"Have you talked to your daughter, Ms. Hyman?"

She bopped her head the way Eastern Indians do when they say 'yes'. "No, but I'm sure she's OK. Isn't she? I mean she's with her boyfriend, right? That's what the sheriff said. I mean, I was hurt—I'd driven all that way to get her . . ."

"That seems to be the common belief, but if it was true, wouldn't she try to contact you? Her mother? You know, to let you know she was okay? Meredith seemed like a caring person to me. Like someone who would want her mother, at least, to know she was okay."

She chewed on that thought a few minutes. "She is! She is caring. Wow. I should probably go home. I mean that's where she'll try to call me, right?"

"Yeah. Or her father."

She looked up at me: "Doug? I hope he never finds her. He'll ruin her life."

"I'm a little confused," I admitted, "didn't you ask him to find her? Isn't that how I ended up in this fine pickle?"

"Ahhh." I'd befuddled her once again.

"It doesn't matter. Can you tell me what happened the night she disappeared?"

"She was gone. I'd driven all the way out from Tahoe, and she was gone. And then I remembered what you said about the caves and . . . Oh golly, I really better go home now, huh?"

"Did you go to the barracks and verify for yourself that she was gone?"

"They were all gone. I've got to go now." She tried to stand but then fell back into the beanbag.

"All of them?"

"Yeah. The room was empty—even the blankets were gone from the beds. I think I fainted, because the next thing I remember I was on the floor and the guard was telling me I had to leave."

"You had to leave—why?"

"I don't know," she sobbed, "he just said he'd put gas in my car and that I had to leave. Then he walked me outside the gate and told me to get into the car and go away. I've never been so freaked out in all my life! I told the sheriff but he . . ."

"You told the sheriff that all the girls had disappeared?" I prompted.

"Yes. No. I don't remember. My car blew up. Then there was that funny-looking man, the sheriff. We went out there in the morning, but the tunnel, the tunnel was all covered up," she sobbed. "Then he told me Merry had left with a boyfriend. He told me it was the only logical thing. And stupid me! I didn't even think that she'd try to call me." She rose to her feet. "I've got to go. I don't know why I didn't figure this out sooner—she's been trying to call me while I've been waiting for that stupid car to get fixed! What's wrong with me—why didn't I figure that out?"

"Shock probably."

"Didn't Doug send a car? He was supposed to send a car."

"Yes—it's back in town. Creamo has it."

"Creamo? He hates me. He's probably rigged it so it will blow up! I know what. I'll just borrow Sal's car."

With that she was up and gone and so was I. As fast as my short legs would carry me, out the front door, past the bouncer, and to the waiting cab. My half hour was up.

CHAPTER 19

I HAD A ROOM WITH A BATH, which was a luxury at the Ely Hotel. It faced the street, which might be a problem in the middle of summer when cowboys came into town to whoop it up at the Iron Bull across the street, but on a Thursday night in October, only the sound of an occasional car whizzing through town broke the quiet.

Before hitting the hay, I'd talked Creamo into trying the Basque restaurant down the street from the hotel. He was angry with me for going out to Longley's by myself. Angry, because in his mind, the trip had been a waste of time. I disagreed. I'd found out that Peterson was lying. All of the girls disappeared that night, not just Meredith Hyman. I'd also learnt that the old man in Steptoe was probably Leticia Honeywell's grandfather. Another lead. That didn't change his mind. Nothing Sabrina Hyman ever said could be trusted.

"Isn't Basque food spicy?" he growled, changing the subject.

"Basque food is not in the least bit spicy," I assured him. "Besides, a bit of garlic is good for digestion."

Of course, I didn't tell him that at Basque restaurants all the guests are expected to sit at one long table and pass large bowls of mashed potatoes, garlic-roasted leg of lamb, and buttered peas back and forth boarding house style. If I had, I doubt he would have gone. He'd lived on his own for too long, his circle of acquaintances shrinking as they retired and left Vegas, and he didn't want new ones. Friends weren't a renewable resource in his mind.

We'd lucked into a weekly tradition at the restaurant: "Boys night out" for a trio of WWII flying daredevils who'd retired to eastern Nevada after learning that it was a place where aeronautical regulations were laxly enforced, or not at all. This meant that a gent with a minor heart condition or failing eyesight was still at liberty to fly to his heart's content. All over the skies! Unshackled from regulations that were pure, unadulterated age discrimination! They'd been Air Force captains and then, after the war, commercial pilots, thus were used to flying in the very worst conditions! They vowed to fly until the bitter end, sitting across from us all rosy-cheeked and twinkle-eyed from the day's adventures. Among the three, we heard a bounty of rollicking tales while trying in vain to keep up with the avalanche of comfort food arriving from the kitchen: asparagus, peas, macaroni salad, mashed potatoes, lamb stew.

During one of the few lulls in the conversation, I slipped in a question about the terrain behind Cavalry Peak. They exchanged glances, and then the pilot in the middle, a man with the squarest jawbone I'd ever seen, replied:

"May I ask, mellifluous one, why you want to know about the miasma behind our legendary monadnock?"

"Captain Wug, Cavalry is not a monadnock," his friend interrupted. "Ayes Rock, now there's a monadnock. I have to apologize for my buddy, young lady. After the war Wug here flew the Far East route for PanAm, meaning he had, ah, far too much air time on his hand and, apparently, only the dictionary to read." The second pilot looked like Madison Avenue's ideal of the aging pilot, still handsome, manly, and self-assured, while the third sported a Mark Twain mustache and bushy black eyebrows that almost obscured his coal-in-the-snow eyes.

"I take exception to that mendacious slander," Captain Wug roared.

"Take exception all you please. Yesterday Hank and I were treated to a litany of obscure words beginning with the letter L and now it appears we're on to M! Isn't that right?"

"Lord God, I'm afraid so," Hank concurred.

"You must forgive my meritorious comrades their resistance to melioration," Captain Wug interjected. "Referring to Cavalry as a monadnock is hardly a grievous malapropism. However, my curiosity remains unabated—why is a charming young lady such as yourself interested in that area of mystifying moraines?"

"Should I tell them?" I asked Creamo.

"No." He'd shrunken back into his shell like a tortoise with gas.

"I'm a romance novelist. Isabella Candlelight is my nom de plume."

"Oh Lord," Creamo groaned.

"How delightful!" Captain Wug exclaimed. "An authoress."

"I'm doing research for my next project – a love story about a young cavalryman and the Indian princess he meets after falling into an underground cave. I'm thinking of setting it in the wilderness area behind Cavalry Peak."

I could hear Creamo belching by my side, but he didn't say a word. The pilots exchanged glances, and then Captain Wug began:

"Holy Ministries of Mythography. Why that area in particular?"

"Oh, I remember as a young girl visiting some of the old forts—Churchill and Storey—and thinking how lonely the cavalrymen must have been, out here in this desolate land far from home."

"I see. Tell me, my dear, have you ever heard of the Bermuda Triangle or any of the other vile vortices malefic to man or even the strongest monocoque?"

"You mean the area behind the mountain is like the Bermuda Triangle?"

"Aye, it is," Hank confirmed. "I've flown through all the so-called 'vile vortices', and that area is the worst."

"You mollycoddled milquetoast! The Devil's Sea has pulled dozens of planes from the skies and sunken thousands of ships, while the area behind Cavalry Peak has swallowed but a pittance of woefully misguided pilots."

"Ha—that's because Cavalry Peak's not a major trade route like the Devil's Sea," Hank snorted. "It'd be a goddamn different story if it were. I once tried to take a shortcut to St. George straight through that area. Last time I ever made that mistake! I ended up—and I don't know how!—over the goddamn Bonneville Salt Flats. I swear to God, young lady, I had not been drinking. Captain Kit, you remember?"

The still handsome Captain Kit nodded his head. "I seem to remember you interrupted some crazy TV show they were filming out there. Crash landed in the middle of a set!"

"It was a movie, not a damn television show, and it was not a crash landing. I guided Mother down nice and smooth. Hey," he stopped. The server had just brought forth the apple pie. "Where's the ice cream? You can't have pie à la mode without the mode!"

"No ice cream?!" Captain Wug huffed, feigning indignation. "We'll not tolerate this outrage!"

"Ice Cream! Ice Cream!" The other diners chanted until a bowl filled with round scoops of homemade French-vanilla ice cream arrived. It was quickly passed around the table by the rowdy diners, who forked and then plopped their share onto steaming pie.

After we'd finished, Captain Hank wiped his mustache with a napkin and then remarked offhandedly, "You know, a young fellow was at the airstrip asking about that area a few days ago. As I recall, he brought his boat down a bit shaky, like he was a pup—yup, a pup in a mighty-fine Cessna. Once he settled, he walked over all friendly-like and proceeded to question us."

"He was a federal agent, maybe FBI, I'm pretty sure," Captain Kit replied. "I can smell those buggers from miles away. He's evidently not used to landing on a rutted bit of asphalt like the three of us, but I don't think he was a pup. No sir, he was probably in his late thirties. He wanted to know about the old mines, you know, if any of them were still active. We let him take a gander at some of our maps."

"He asked about that old fort too," Captain Hank added. "You know, Fort Palmer. Nice fellow for a fed. Think he said his name was Lopinsky. Louie Lopinsky."

"Did he kind of look like a hobbit?" I asked, struggling for words to describe the man who'd visited me at the hospital. "You know, round faced, not very tall."

"A hobbit, huh?" Captain Kit chuckled. "I guess that'd describe him about as good as anything, although I always assumed that if I ran into a real live hobbit, he'd look just like Hank here, you know, with a big old mustache and eyebrows so long and squirrelly that you could barely see his eyes."

This trickle of mild slander led to a flood of good-natured teasing from which it was difficult to extricate any of the three pilots without seeming rude. Finally the cook appeared to thank us all for coming, our cue to leave, as the restaurant was now closed. Thank you very much; now pay and leave. But before the pilots took off for home and wives, they proposed we meet them the next day at their airstrip. "We have topographical maps," they explained, "of the entire area. They'll tell you everything you want to know."

Creamo thanked them but I could tell he had no desire to mull over topographical maps with a trio of old geezers, as he called them. In his mind it was a fait accompli. Young girl runs off with boyfriend. Happens every day.

"Look, Butters. You might as well scoot on back to Vegas. I'm going to have this thing wrapped up by tomorrow."

"Maybe I will." I replied. "At least I know why that man came to visit me in the hospital."

"What man?"

"Oh, just before your boss ordered me back to Enev, some guy popped into my hospital room expecting me to recognize him. I thought he might be some kind of cop, but I guess he's with the FBI."

"I saw that guy. FBI? No."

"Maybe he's investigating Meredith's disappearance."

"Nope, that's not it."

"Well, then maybe he's investigating the bat-poop researchers. But I wonder why he was trying to find the Nova. That doesn't make any sense."

"Who cares?" Creamo sighed as he headed for the Iron Bull for a nightcap.

Outside the wind howled, whistling through drafty windows and disrupting the power supply. The lights flickered and then dimmed, filling the room with shades of grey like an old photo. Somewhere in the desert, young girls serviced truckers. And Butters sits in an existentialist funk, I thought, doing nothing. Then I had an idea. It was late but worth a try.

CHAPTER 20

THE CALLBACKS CREAMO HAD EXPECTED the night before came while we were eating breakfast, and like a good and trusty hound, he immediately rose to take them. By the time he returned, his eggs (sunnyside up) looked as appetizing as puddles of yellow plastic, but he picked at them anyway, as he grumbled. Preliminary analysis of the tire treads led to a plant in Chicago specializing in custom tires for military vehicles: large-scale, four-wheel drive trucks. "There aren't any military bases within 500 miles!" he grumbled.

"How about all those boyfriends?"

"Dead ends. So far. There could always be one we don't know about."

"How about Dr. Gnecht? Did you get any news back about him?"

Creamo scowled. He liked his mysteries to be straightforward and not filled with underground caves, whacky biologists, and girlish folderol. He eyeballed the rigid piece of bacon in his hand and then gave me his steno pad. "Look for yourself," he said, "if you can read my writing."

Alexander Lucian Gnecht, PhD. 15 y w/ Dept of Agr, Pubs/Sc Amer/ Natl Geo (bats disords.) Black-filed.

"So he does actually work for the government. Will wonders never cease?" I sighed. "What does 'black-filed' mean?"

"It's a term the feds sometimes use to describe an internal investigation," Creamo explained. "He must have gone rogue and that's why the FBI is here."

"I wonder why the department sent out a couple of interns to work with him if he was under investigation. Any mention of when he was black-filed?" I asked.

"Evidently that information is in the goddamned black file."

"Figures. No psych?"

"Yeah, but you had that one nailed—no family, no friends, several referrals for counseling, the whole shebang. They're going to send us a fax as soon as the secretary gets into the office. Dimwits can't figure out how to use the machine," he chuckled, looking over at me impishly. "There was something interesting about your buddy Winnie Peterson, née Ralston."

"Yeah?"

"I think you're in for a surprise."

"Please—no suspense. Just spit it out."

"Read—it's on the next page."

He watched me flip the page, chuckling at my expression when I'd finished reading. "See. Not what you expected I bet."

"Don't be silly—I'm a trained psychiatrist!"

"And I'm an ex-cop."

"So the sheriff has to be lying."

"It would seem so."

"I mean, he has been living in these parts for awhile, right?"

"Yup. That's what he claims."

"Shall we call him on it?"

"Not unless you want to hear another line of bull."

"What are you going to do?" I asked. "If you want my opinion . . ."

"No thanks—you're leaving town, right?"

"You should try to track down the three girls Winnie Peterson says she released. Come on, it should be easy enough to contact the mental hospital." He ignored me. I continued anyway. "And I'm pretty sure the crazy old coot at the store in Steptoe is Leticia Honeywell's grandfather. If you can track down at least two, one of them should lead you to Meredith Hyman, if indeed she did escape."

He wasn't paying attention to anything I said.

"What do I have to do in this place to get more coffee?"

"Well, here's a suggestion. Get up and get it yourself."

He scowled. "Gotta get my own booze; gotta get my own coffee. This place is a real shit hole." He leaned backwards in his seat and shouted at the waitress. "How do I get a cup of coffee in this place?"

The waitress had her back to us, chatting with someone who'd just entered the café. She turned slowly and sneered in our direction. Behind her stood the jocular, loquacious, and often indecipherable Captain Wug. He gave us a wave and, taking the coffee pot from the waitress' hand, made his way to our table.

"May I join your reticular ruminations?" he asked. He was dressed in a bomber jacket, trousers that looked like they'd been made from parachute material, well-worn boots that laced above his ankles, and an old leather helmet.

"Sure, sit," I replied. "You just saved Creamo from a lapful of boiling hot java!"

He laughed heartily, pulling up a chair, "I believe you're right! In fact, if I were the two of you, I'd be having breakfast down at Casa Maria tomorrow morning." He looked first at me and then at Creamo, "I hope I'm not interrupting . . ."

"We were just wondering how a runner-up to Miss Nevada and the wife of a local war hero could have ended up as an administrator out at Enev. Perhaps you know."

"You've got me half-baked with mulberry sauce, my dear. I've only been out here a few years. Not nearly long enough to acquaint myself with this area's finer specimens of womanhood." He paused before continuing. "However . . . if the war hero you're talking about is Ward Peterson, then, yes, I did hear something. I won't pretend that nasty rumors don't fly about these parts faster than fleas on mule deer, but . . . I try not to listen, not because of any sort of moral imperative, mind you, but because the missus would skin me alive if I did! She is the finer person."

"Now you've got my imagination piqued. What happened to the war hero?"

"Oh it's nasty stuff and completely hearsay. The facts, which I don't mind repeating, are that no one has seen him for years. He lives on what remains of the Peterson ranch and never comes into town. His wife lives at the girls' reformatory—some wagging mouths say it's her way of doing penance for sins of the past. There, I've given you enough of a clue."

"Women," Creamo growled.

"I expected to see you two at the strip this morning. Weren't you interested in the terrain behind Cavalry Peak, you know, as a possible setting for your epic saga of undying love?"

"I've changed my mind—I write romance novels; not science fiction."

"Oh, what a pity!" he sighed. "I thought I'd fly you two out there myself, for the price of a full tank of gas that is. My blushing bride tires of the scenery and demands, ever so sweetly of course, that we adjourn to our winter abode, by commercial air, unfortunately. So, this may be my last flight of the season before I say sayonara to my sweet mistress."

"Go for it, Butters," Creamo chuckled, pulling twenties from his wallet. "I can't go. I gotta wait here for Hyman's call. I tell you what, I'll even let you take the camera in case you happen to spot something interesting—like maybe the entrance to the caves of Oswando Land, or whatever that place is called."

"Thank you, but statistically, small airplanes are more dangerous than . . ." I began.

"Statistically, anything can kill you," Creamo reminded me. "You're not afraid, are you?"

"Not that I know of. I've never been up in a small plane."

"Then go. It's a piece of cake. Just like being in the big ones."

The airstrip was a few miles west of town. It was basically a rutted strip of asphalt running parallel to a two-lane highway. The hangar was about the size of a barn and housed a rusty coke machine, cots for overnight visitors, and a walled-off section used as an office, wherein pilots could access radar equipment, topographical maps, and unsolicited advice proffered by 'the Colonel', an old-timer who took to the air these days only occasionally. There were maybe a half-dozen small planes parked haphazardly outside the hangar, looking well loved and used.

Before we set off for his plane, Captain Wug perused the radar. The skies looked clear. Excellent weather for a flight.

"Don't we have to file a flight plan?" I asked.

"Already done," Captain Wug replied. "Generally the Colonel gives me and the boys a pass; however, since we will be flying over an area Search and Rescue won't enter unless they know for a fact you've crashed, I duly complied."

"That's reassuring," I quipped.

What have I gotten myself into, I thought as we walked through the planes. They all looked so flimsy, like they were made from a kit by some high-school kid. My spirits lightened momentarily when I spotted a canary-yellow four-door model, with shiny silver propellers and a brand-spanking-new vibe. Oh, please let that be the captain's plane, I thought. Please, please, please.

It was not. The captain's pride and joy was a biplane: the type flown in vintage air shows, the type you imagine piloted by a lunatic in long purple scarves, flying upside down while buzzing the crowds.

"Where are the parachutes?" I asked, as he helped me onboard, the upper wing so close to my head that I could touch it. The worn seats were not built for comfort; the windshield was pitted from years of desert flight.

He started up the propeller through an odd bit of sorcery involving several knobs and doohickeys. "This is a Polikarpov Po2 biplane, my fair wordsmith. We won't be flying high enough for a parachute to serve any purpose other than as a shroud. During the war these planes were known as the Whistling Death."

"During the war? This plane was flown during the war?"

"Yes, dear, by our then good buddies the Russians. Russian women in particular. But never fear; she has a relatively new Ash 61R engine so she's like an old pro with a tightened vagina, if you'll pardon my French. Plus she's got sturdy shoes and can set down in inhospitable terrains, always a good thing for flights beyond the Space Man."

"What is the Space Man, exactly? A hieroglyph?"

"A hieroglyph? No, my dear, it's a tor or perhaps a stone run, we'd have to ask Professor Hank for the proper geological term, a rock formation that, from above, resembles a child's drawing of a man with an extra large head, like an astronaut or deep-sea diver."

Suddenly we were rolling, bouncing on the uneven surface as we passed the other planes. I had a strong urge to jump, but the thought of how ridiculous and foolish I would look stopped me. I can do this, I told myself. Piece of cake.

The captain continued, "There are those who absolutely refuse to see the Space Man for what it is, arguing that it must be the creation of man or alien or even God!"

"Like the people who see the image of the Virgin Mary in a shriveled potato."

"Exactly. You'll see—we'll fly over it but not much further beyond. Not that I put much store in the rantings of my superstitious colleagues but because, as I said, SAR will refuse to come find us if we get lost too deep in that territory."

We'd reached the runway, a black strip now shimmering like a mirage in the sunlight. "See anything?" he asked.

"What do you mean? I see power lines at the end of the runway. Are you sure we're taking off in the right direction?"

"Other planes, my dear, a flock of birds. Maybe even, a UFO!"

"I see power lines dangling . . ."

"Say good-bye to your earthly womb, Mademoiselle Candlelight of the Romance Genre and prepare to be reborn in the sky, free of all petty concerns, free to dance with the clouds! Oh! I have slipped the surly bonds of earth, and danced the skies on laughter-silvered wings; sunward I've climbed, and joined the tumbling mirth of sun-split clouds, —and done a hundred things I have not dreamed of," he sang as we picked up a little speed but not nearly enough to be airborne. My heart was pounding, my hands sweaty. Tears squeezed from my eyes. I was so frightened, I couldn't even talk.

A few feet from the end of the runway, he jerked back on the throttle and up we rose, not smoothly like a jumbo jet, but like a roller coaster, up and down and finally skimming over the hot, buzzing wires.

"Holy Shit!" I mumbled. "I could have touched those power lines!"

"Hang on to your stomach, my dear," he uttered with unadulterated glee. "We're not clear yet—we've got an exhilarating half roll coming up; otherwise we'll slam right into the side of Rattlesnake Mountain."

"Exhilarating? My ass! Who designed this runway? It's more like an obstacle course."

"Nonsense! Try landing a cargo plane on Lindbergh Field. Now there's an obstacle course."

Below I could see jackrabbits scurrying this way and that, perhaps thinking a giant hungry hawk was above them, and then, without warning, the right wings dropped and I was sideways, face-to-face with the desert floor. The engine revved loudly as the plane rolled in a wide half circle, its shadow flitting along the desert floor like a ballerina pirouetting across the stage. The sudden awareness of my body as a shadow provoked a twitch of existential angst. Something intrinsic to me had escaped and now laughed from its place of relative security at my precarious predicament. I felt like frigging Peter Pan.

"You've got to admit. It's better than sex," Captain Wug sighed as the wings leveled off. We were heading east into the sun, following the highway leading back into town.

"I can't remember sex," I muttered. Both of my armpits were drenched. My stomach lay far behind on the dusty tarmac. Sex was the last thing on my mind.

"Pshaw! A lovely lass like you? Perhaps that's why you've chosen the romance genre . . ."

"Before you go any further, Dr. Freud, I should confess. I'm not really a romance novelist. God forbid. The most anal-retentive CPA on the planet could write a more believable romance novel than me! I'm actually trying to find a girl who disappeared from the girls' reformatory four days ago. At one time I was considered an expert in, well, abnormal psychology, which is what got me into this pickle. My real name is Fi Butters."

"I see."

"Well, there's an old cemetery at Fort Palmer and just above it, a mine tunnel that was boarded over, but somehow the young ladies—inmates if you want to call them that—have pried open the boards and have been using the tunnel to escape. But I can't figure out where to. One of miscreants claimed under hypnosis that the tunnel leads to a sinkhole. Have you seen anything like that?"

"A sinkhole? That's usually the type of thing you'd expect to find in the Yucatan or Florida."

"Yes, I'd considered that she might have been describing a repressed childhood memory . . ."

"Sinkholes would be quite unusual out here, unless . . ."

"Unless?"

"The subterranean peculiarities of this area are legendary, my dear, making it impossible to catalogue the many oddities, the many strange occurrences."

"There are a lot of old mining operations in this area, right?"

"Mining is what made most of Nevada, mining and the railroads."

"Anyone actively working out at any of the old mines?"

"Hmm," Captain Wug sighed, "hmm."

"Anyone who might be working out of a pair of those aluminum trailers?"

You'd think the desert would be more scenic from a small plane but it isn't. You see things from the air that you miss whizzing by in a car—backyard garbage dumps, the half-eaten carcasses of cows, ponds fluorescent with pollutants. Things people want to hide. It's like the ultimate form of snoopery, peeking in folks' backyards from above.

"Spanish Spring!" he exclaimed after a few stale moments. "I heard that someone'd dragged a pair of Airstreams and a generator out there. No one seemed to know what they were doing, but it was the site of flourishing enterprise at one time. Why don't we fly over and do a reconnaissance?"

"There's only one problem with that plan. The men working out there are not only armed, but they're paranoid."

"How do you know that, my dear?"

"I ran into them while I was checking out the mine tunnel."

"And you think the girl may have too?"

"Could be. I'm kind of curious to see where exactly it is."

"Then by happy circumstance, we are in the perfect machine. We'll cut the engines on approach and glide over the valley."

"Is that safe?"

"That's the beauty of Polikarpov! You know what it was used for, don't you?"

Of course, I did not.

"Aha. Well, my dear, at the end of the war, with able-bodied men in short demand, barely trained but fearless Russian women took to the sky in these old crop dusters! Their mission—to steal over the German borders in the wee hours of the morning and drop explosives on sleep-deprived, shell-shocked soldiers. The eerie whistling of the bracing wires was the last sound those poor sods heard before the bombs dropped."

"This plane was a bomber? It doesn't look big enough to drop water balloons from."

Captain Wug laughed. "They were nuisance bombs. A bit of blasting powder and nails—firecrackers! Able to start fires, nothing more. But that was enough, my dear. Enough to prevent those sniffling cowards from getting a decent night's sleep. And the fact that the planes were piloted by women and not men! Ha, ha, ha! Shriveled their egos! The mighty Teutonic warriors, the heros of the Third Reich, prime examples of the Master Race, quivering in their bunks at night because of a few daring, barely trained babushkas in biplanes! Ha, ha, ha!"

Captain Wug reveled in this story for several minutes more, the memory of these fine specimens of womanhood, these Amazons of the Air, who evidently captured both his undying admiration and seemingly endless imagination decades before, still stirred him into such a froth that I worried whether his heart could take it. The only thing that brought him back to the present day was the sight of Calvary Peak now looming on our horizon, its summit shrouded by a petticoat of wispy cumuli.

The notorious Space Man was, I must admit, a disappointing sight, a pattern of rocks that, with a huge amount of imagination, could be said to resemble a man with a very big head and octopus-like legs and arms. It didn't inspire any fear or even curiosity in me. It did, however, sit at the end of a long flat plateau that, like so many desert outcroppings, reminded me of the outer battlements of a medieval castle.

"I see what you mean about the Space Man."

He chuckled, "I've heard there are striations on the head of the Space Man that upon laborious inspection detail the end of days."

"Oh yeah? If you say so."

He laughed again.

As soon as we cleared the plateau, the vast expanse of wilderness behind Cavalry Peak unfolded; stony mountains barren of green, between which glacier-forged gorges lay stripped bare like stone quarries, waiting for the hapless to wander into uninvited and be defeated. Over a range of purple-toothed peaks to the south hung a worrisome umbrella of dark purple clouds.

Captain Wug scowled as the umbrella rapidly changed in shape, bubbling higher into the sky and sending long fingers of stratus streaking towards us like pointing fingers.

"For the love of Sassafras! What hellish maelstrom gave birth to that audacious squall?" Captain Wug snarled as he reported our coordinates to the Colonel.

"There's nothing on the radar," was the garbled response.

"Balderdash—I can see it plain as the nose on my face."

The garble quickly changed to static. We'd lost radio contact.

"Perhaps it's best if we don't dillydally over Spanish Springs," the captain sighed.

"Forget Spanish Springs! I've seen tornadoes that looked less deadly than those clouds."

"Oh nonsense. A pilot is always at his best in inclement weather! Besides, we're almost there. In fact, I think I see it now. 'In Xanadu did Kubla Khan, a stately pleasure dome decree, where Alph, the sacred river, ran through caverns measureless to man down to a sunless sea.'"

Spanish Spring hardly resembled a pleasure dome. What was left of the mine clung to the side of the mountain in tatters and rust, blasted by sand. At one time, it had been a sizable operation with conveyer belts and trestles—all the latest and greatest, now ransacked by looters, thrill seekers, and the elements. But the sight seemed to inspire the captain as he cut the engines:

"But oh! That deep romantic chasm
which slanted down the green hill athwart a cedar cover!
A savage place! As holy and enchanted as e'er
beneath a waning moon was haunted by woman
wailing for her demon-lover!
And from this chasm, with ceaseless turmoil seething,
as if this earth in fast thick pants were breathing,
a mighty fountain momently was forced:
amid whose swift half-intermitted burst huge fragments
vaulted like rebounding hail."

He stopped his recitation. "Can you hear it? The whistling of the bracing wires, the whistling death."

"I think we're about to fall into that mighty chasm, Kubla Khan," I quipped. "Can't you feel us dropping, and there's no trapeze net beneath us, you know?"

He chuckled. "What you're feeling is the barometric pressure falling," he claimed as we came within view of two Airstream trailers. "Ho—there they are! Hiding behind the old mill, for shame. I wonder how they managed to drag those wretched sardine cans all the way out here. Take a gander, my dear—is this the place? "

I took a quick and nauseating glance over the wing. "Yup. There's Gnecht's jeep. Listen, I don't want to sound like a Nervous Nelly but shouldn't we be restarting the engines?"

"Shortly, shortly," he promised as we made a slow turn. "I take it that your previous experience in the air has been limited to somniferous treks cross-country in a wide-body, flying bar. Such a pity! This is true flight! Gliding on the wind, through wispy clouds from which the seraphim observe the petty misdeeds of the mortals."

He was right, of course. This was real flying. That other experience, of sitting cramped in an aisle seat waiting for Coke and peanuts, listening to babies cry or the man next to you snore, the sound of the jet engines purring steadily as you breathe recycled air, that was for cowards, for wimps unwilling to look death in the face and sneer, for dullards who do not wish to boldly go where no man has gone before. In other words, people exactly like me, "I'm not ready to play footsies with angels. Could you just do me a favor and start the bloody engine?"

"I was preparing to do precisely that," he claimed, twisting his knobs and doo-hickeys. "Then we'll head due west—out of the path of that juggernaut. Look at how it's grown! My goodness—you might get a picture of that, my dear. Proof that we're not telling another fish tale."

The first attempt to restart the engine failed. It was the wind he claimed. It was hitting us from the wrong angle. He turned so that the wind was behind us. The propeller began to sputter. But not for long. "We're going to have to ditch," the captain sighed. "Let's hope we can reach the plateau."

* * *

When he saw the storm approach, Louie Lopinsky ran down the hill to the safety of 'The Tank', which is what he called the gas-guzzling four-wheel drive he'd rented in Ely. It stretched his budget, he later told me, but he was sure his publisher wouldn't mind, even though he hadn't been offered a signed contract—yet.

In the process of stumbling through the weeds, he'd gathered many little prickles in his socks, stinging him around the ankle like a colony of fire ants. He was trying to remove them when he heard sputtering overhead. A small plane in trouble. He waited several minutes expecting to hear an explosion but there was none. Curious, he thought, were they able to land? The terrain for as far as he could see was hilly and rock-strewn. Except for the long flat plateau. Perhaps the pilot had been able to restart his engine and avert the necessity to put down, but a little voice whispered, no. The plane had gone down. Then the downpour hit.

"You're the man who came to see me in the hospital," was my first comment upon seeing Louie Lopinsky again. The captain had broken his collar bone following our landing. Any movement jiggled bone shards, causing them to dig into his flesh, but the fact that he'd been injured not during the landing but after, leaping from the cabin in the windstorm to secure the plane, was a hard pill to swallow. Not nearly as hard to swallow, however, as the necessity to ditch in the first place. Apparently, it isn't that easy to cut the engine of a plane and then restart it after coasting several hundred yards, even if you used that technique dozens of times against the Germans with stunning success. Still, despite his agony, I was sure that the resulting tales from this adventure would more than compensate.

"I sure am surprised to see you again so soon," Lopinsky said as he helped me immobilize the captain's shoulder. "I thought you'd still be in the hospital or at least recuperating. I didn't expect you to plop out of the sky in front of me!"

"I certainly didn't either." Now that I knew he was an FBI agent I was dying to ask Lopinsky who he was investigating, but, not knowing the captain's medical history, the priority was to get him taken care of first. Questions later.

"The plateau is pretty steep," Lopinsky said, "I can leave you two here and go get help…"

"No," the captain and I both said in unison.

"We'll just take it slowly," I promised. Luckily Captain Wug was in reasonable shape, and, save an occasional twinge of pain, managed to stay upright until we got him down the slippery hill to Lopinsky's car.

"What's your name, Captain?" Lopinsky asked as we drove down the creek bed. "As soon as I get a signal on my ham radio here, I'll tell whomever I reach to contact your family. Mighty useful things, these radios. You wouldn't catch me out in the desert without one."

"Wilson Umberto Grayson," the captain admitted, slowly. "Young man, you're indeed a scholar . . . and a gentleman. Do assure my blushing bride that Natasha has only a few bumps and bruises. I fully intend to . . . um, fly her off the plateau as soon as I've been diapered and patched." Each word required breath and came with pain.

"I'm sure she'll be comforted by that thought!" I chuckled.

Once we got radio contact, we were directed to a clinic on the outskirts of town where the enchanting Mrs. Grayson awaited our arrival, a smile on her face but worry in her eyes. She looked about twenty years younger than the old goat she was married to. Upon seeing her, he put on a brave face, greeting her thusly, "Alas, my ravishing temptress . . . my nubile bride . . . never fear. I'll not let my bumps and bruises interrupt our . . um, nightly celebrations of your delicious nether regions!" And then, thankfully, the nursing crew wheeled him away.

CHAPTER 21

AFTER WE LEFT THE CLINIC, Lopinksi gave me a lift to downtown Ely and bought me a therapeutic hot fudge sundae at the Dairy Queen. I was wrong about him, of course. He wasn't an FBI agent, and what's worse, he thought it endlessly entertaining I even had such a silly notion. "My students will get a kick out of that story," he laughed.

"If you're not a federal agent, then why were you waving a badge around at the airstrip?" I asked.

"Waving a badge? I don't have a badge, but I do have a library card. University of North Carolina staff member with special access to vaulted manuscripts." He pulled out the contents of his wallet and spread them over the sticky Formica table, to prove that he was as lethal as the boy next door. He'd opted for fries instead of a sundae, dumping them in a lake of blood-red catsup and sprinkling them with an extra dose of salt. The two of us were poster children for unhealthy eating, but I didn't care.

He thought a minute. "They probably jumped to that conclusion because my plane still has government tags. You see, I bought it a few weeks ago at auction and have been too preoccupied preparing for my trip to handle the legalities."

I still wasn't convinced. College professors generally don't make enough money to take up flying as a hobby.

"So, tell me about this theory you have regarding the Civil War?"

"Haven't you ever heard that it's bad luck to talk about a book until it's practically at the publishers?"

"I know fiction writers are leery talking about their work but . . . history professors?"

"History walks the fine line between fiction, folklore and fact, don't you think? Here, listen to this," he ordered, pulling a folded piece of paper from his coat pocket.

There are glittering caves wherein torches are kindled and men walk on the sandy floors under the echoing domes, wherein gems and crystals and veins of precious ores glint in the polished walls; and the light glows through folded marble, shell-like, translucent as living hands.

"Sounds like Tolkien," I said. "The description of Lothlorien, if I remember correctly."

"Yes, but this was written before Tolkien was born," he explained. "This is a copy of a letter to Reverend Simon Olivore from his son, Major Sebastian Olivore, circa 1860s."

Sebastian Olivore. So his words had found and beguiled again. "How did you stumble on his letters?"

"I was cataloging a bequest to the university, documents found in the attic of one of our illustrious Confederate widows, who just happened to be the sister of Reverend Olivore. At first I didn't think too much about them. But later, I began to question why a battalion of the Eleventh Cavalry was stationed in eastern Nevada during the final days of the war."

"I don't understand why that would be unusual. They were there to protect the stagecoaches, right?"

"During the Indian Wars, the cavalry generally consisted of bands of local vigilantes, hell bent on harassing the natives. Besides, Lincoln needed every man he could get his hands on, so why send a division west? It didn't make any sense."

"So Lincoln himself ordered the Eleventh Cavalry out to Fort Palmer?"

"Well, that part is hard to prove. That's why I'd like to see the Major's journal. His early letters to his father were understandably guarded, and the latter ones didn't make much sense, so I'm hoping his journal . . ."

"Well, Professor. I've read it and most of it is, well, prosy. The last entries suggest some sort of psychotic breakdown."

"You said the same thing in the hospital." He paused before continuing. "I think the Major saw something he wasn't supposed to. That's why his letters suddenly stopped coming and why his family was unable to find out what happened to him." He dangled a soggy fry in my direction. "Care for a fry?"

"No thanks—I like my fries dipped in catsup, not drowning in it. Besides, I'm a Cheetos lady."

"I know." He hesitated. "You really don't remember talking to me in the hospital, do you?"

"I only remember you telling me something about the Nova—I thought you were a cop."

"My poor ego."

I had to stop for a minute and think. It had been so long that I couldn't tell. Was this man flirting with me? I had to admit the way he wiggled his fries in the catsup, raised them dripping with sticky sweetness to his lips, and slurped them down his gullet, humming with pleasure like a dewy-eyed seal with an oyster, made me tingle. You gotta love a man who relishes eating.

"Ego, smeego, I had short-term amnesia for the first two and a half days. I didn't even remember my own doctor."

"Really? You were so charming."

"So I've heard. Evidently when my brain functions like a sieve, my social skills improve to the point that I'm reasonably tolerable. Can you tell me what we talked about, at least?"

He reached over and patted my free hand. "It'd be my pleasure," he began, with just a hint of the south under his tongue once again. "You were most obliging—told me about the girls and their fascination with this young man—I believe you had a psychological term for it which presently evades me."

"Heavens—there's a psychological term for everything! But how did . . ."

"How did I know about the journal? My first night in town I rented a room in the boarding house across from the police station. That was last Saturday night."

"The night the girls disappeared."

"And the night Sabrina Hyman's jaguar blew up in front of the police station."

"Ah . . . So you heard the story from her?"

"Yup. In bits and pieces, as we tried to calm her down. What luck, hey?" He paused. "Say, who's that fellow watching us from the window? Your husband?"

Creamo stood just outside the Diary Queen, the jacket of his collar rolled up against the cold, smoking a cigarette, and looking in our direction uncomfortably.

"That's Detective Creamo, my bodyguard," I explained waving him in. He shook his head no. "Obviously he hasn't been doing a very good job guarding my body but he has perfected the look, don't you think?"

"Bogart couldn't have played it better," he said looking down at his watch. "Shoot. I didn't realize it was so cotton-pickin' late. I've got to go. Expecting a call from my publisher."

"Wait a minute. How did you track me to the hospital?"

"Oh, that would be Sabrina Hyman again. She thought you had the journal and that it would lead to her daughter's whereabouts. So I flew down to Vegas, on her dime, of course. But she wouldn't go with me."

"Afraid of flying?"

"Afraid of her ex. Now, I really do have to go."

"Wait. I have a lot more questions—"

"Tomorrow."

"I haven't even thanked you for saving my sorry sack of bones."

He smiled boyishly. "It was my pleasure. But alas, my publisher is paying the bills!"

And then he slid out of the DQ and down the street, turning once to flash another grin in my direction, before fading into the shadows. I dug into the bottom of the sundae for any remaining melted chocolate, savoring it slowly, as Creamo ventured cautiously inside to claim me, like some father chaperoning his teenage daughter home from the prom.

"Who's the boyfriend?" he asked, as we shuffled down the wood-planked sidewalk toward the hotel. The night air was icy. There were rumors of snow. If not for Lopinsky, I would still be out there on the plateau with the captain, trying to figure out why the radio wasn't working, hoping someone would fly over and see us, trying to keep my toes warm, starving to death, and probably fighting the frisky old devil off.

"Aren't you going to ask where I've been all this time?"

"Oh, I know all about your accident. This may be a hick town, Butters, but it's full of ham operators. They spread the news faster than a gaggle of old ladies." He started to chuckle. "You know, Hyman cracked up when I told him you actually went up in one of those flying tin cans with some crazy old coot."

"I can believe it."

"I think he has a thing for you, Butters."

"What?"

"Yeah, you amuse him. Like that lady in the Bible. Sharizada? The one who told stories so she wouldn't lose her head."

I almost took the bait. And then I realized the old buzzard was just trying to get my goat. "Ha, ha," I replied, "that's Scheherazade, Mr. Creamo, not Sharizada."

CHAPTER 22

THE ADRENALINE RUSH that had kept me going through the day wore off sometime around midnight, and the result was, in a word (and not a very descriptive word at that) pain. Everything either ached, throbbed, or pinched. The pinching in my neck was the worst; the only position endurable was lying flat on my back. Luckily the hospital staff had insisted I take a bottle of muscle relaxants. Delayed whiplash from the rough landing, they warned. They were right. My neck had been both whipped and lashed, savagely and without mercy, and now rebelled at the thought of doing its job: holding up my head.

By breakfast I was sufficiently numbed to accept Creamo's offer to join him. He had a new theory about what might have happened to Meredith Hyman.

"Oh, please. I'm in too much pain to laugh," I groaned after his recitation. "You've been talking to Sal Longley, haven't you?"

"No I did some more research on the Petersons. Did you know his cousin is Jedediah Watson?"

"Who's that?" I asked. Then as quickly as I closed my trap, the image of a bearded goofball, surrounded by a bevy of farm girls fresh from milking, popped into my mind. "Oh, you mean the polygamist?"

"Yeah. I mean, it's a religious thing with the Mormons, having all those wives, and they start marrying them real young, you know, so they can squeeze out lots of good Mormon babies. Here's the thing: I called that mental hospital yesterday. You know, the one she supposedly sent that little . . ."

I stopped him before he could slip in a racist slur, "Vietnamese girl? Thanh?"

"They have no record of her. Peterson lied to us."

He uttered this with such seriousness, I couldn't stifle my response, a painful chortle. Duh, Creamo, duh.

"Oh goody," I squealed when our food finally arrived: pancakes, eggs, and sausages that could use a bit more browning.

Creamo reached for the antacid tablets he always kept in his shirt pocket. He popped them like candy. Pink and yellow tablets, sometimes a lime green. He chewed them with a vengeance and then washed the debris into the septic tank he called a stomach. Then he started pouring syrup over everything. Runny eggs, sausages, pancakes, everything.

"Here's the thing. If Peterson lied to us about that one gal, then she probably lied about the other two."

"Yeah. Did you talk to the old goat out in Steptoe? I'm pretty sure he's Leticia's grandfather. He could validate whether or not she's been released."

"That was a goddamn waste of time. The store was all boarded up. Closed. It's Winnie Peterson, I tell you. She's done something with those girls."

"Oh great, instead of a teenage boyfriend, the villain is now a deadly broad, that most hackneyed device of dime-store detective novels."

"A deadly broad and her husband!"

Outside the wind made nasty. Tumbleweeds flew past the plate glass window, bouncing over trucks like a flock of turkeys fleeing the hatchet.

"Say, do you think I should ask the waitress to take these sausages back to the kitchen and give them a proper browning? I mean, look at them! I bet they cooked them in one of those gall-darned microwaves. There's nothing in the world worse than an underdone sausage. The fat needs to be sizzling, the skin crispy, otherwise it's like eating lard!"

"Whatever floats your boat," he replied, "I've gotta make some calls."

"You know, I've got another idea. It's a long shot, but heck, you've already got sex traffickers and polygamists on your list of possible suspects, so why not add a few bat biologists to the gumbo? If the girls did escape from Fort Palmer—which, as you said, would not be difficult—it makes sense that they would try to reach the store in Steptoe. Maybe they crossed paths with Cal and Luke and convinced them to drop them at Leticia's grandfather's."

"That's pretty far-fetched. It's a big desert."

"Far fetched? I suppose your idea makes more sense. An evil woman dead set on starting a polygamous family with a group of psychotic girls risks her career—hell, risks prison?"

"Hmm," he mumbled, pushing aside his half-full plate. "I never did like breakfast. It's my least favorite meal."

"That's because it's not served with alcohol. You know, I think this area is getting to you, Creamo. I know it always gets to me. Closed-society thinking often breeds epidemic hysteria. Hey, did I ever tell you the term 'hysteria' comes from the Greek for womb? Yeah, apparently the Greeks thought abnormal uterine movements were responsible for all instances of hysteria, including those that convert to contagious psychogenic events. Ridiculous, hey?"

"As usual, I haven't got a clue what you're talking about, but I suppose it wouldn't hurt to check those guys out," he finally said. "They're armed, right?"

"The guys I ran into in the caves? Yes."

"Hmm. Maybe they were going to hold Merry for ransom, and when she tried to get away, they killed her."

"I don't know. They didn't seem the type."

"Yeah, maybe that Gnecht dude is trying to get back at the government . . ."

"I think it's more likely the two younger men found the girls and were bamboozled into dropping them somewhere. I think I'll go over and talk to the sheriff after breakfast. Find out if he knows where the grandfather might have gone."

I arrived at the sheriff's office just in time to catch him escaping out the door. "Listen, if you want to talk to me, you'll have to keep up—I'm overdue at the courthouse."

"I'm looking for the old guy who runs the convenience store near Steptoe?" I asked. "He seems to have disappeared. I think his last name is Honeywell."

"Fergus? Hell, that's easy. We've got him in the holding cell. We've had him there since last Saturday night."

"Last Saturday night? What'd he do?" I asked.

"Hell if I know."

"You can't lock someone up for almost a week without some sort of reason."

"You can if you're holding him for the feds. Hell, I suppose I could have asked the reason; out here it's generally tax evasion."

"The feds?"

"Yeah they dragged him in the same night Sabrina Hyman's car exploded. So I was, uh, preoccupied. I told my second to handle it. You can talk to him, if you want. Name's Green. You know, I'm only required to hold federal detainees for a week, so if they don't get their act together soon, I'm releasing him. Then you can have him all to yourself."

"I don't want him!"

* * *

When the hotel clerk had no idea where I'd disappeared to, Louie Lopinsky decided to drive out to the modest red-brick medical center on the edge of town to check on Captain Wug, whose clavicle had broken, not merely fractured, requiring a rigid upper body cast that would immobilize his arm for a while. But Captain Wug hadn't allowed the subsequent modicum of discomfort to prevent the constant retelling of his miraculous plateau landing. The staff had been most obliging, but the Professor provided an audience with whom he could revel in the technical details only a fellow pilot could appreciate. Ah, life is so much sweeter when there's an adventure to share.

After they'd exhausted the subject of his miraculous landing, Captain Wug asked Lopinski what sort of clandestine operation had brought him to the apocalyptic side of Cavalry Peak. Lopinsky, having nothing to hide, apparently spoke at depth about his quest.

"Most excellent!" Captain Wug sighed. "Being a native son of the land of Lincoln as I am, I've always had a preternatural interest, bordering on mania, in the War Between the States. You must stay with the missus and me, so I can hear more. I absolutely insist! I can assure you that my blushing bride will be tickled pink to entertain such an esteemed houseguest as yourself."

It was an offer the younger man readily accepted, for he hadn't yet secured that most wonderful of prizes—a contract from the publisher—and so any savings on lodgings was a boon.

"So, what's the plan for today? Captain Wug asked, once the appropriate arrangements were made with Mrs. Grayson.

"Well, I'm going to try to get some photos of the mines on Cavalry Peak," Lopinsky replied.

"Stay away from Spanish Springs," Captain Wug warned. "The worst kind of varmints have taken over the place."

CHAPTER 23

"I THINK HE HAS A CRUSH on you," Captain Wug chuckled.

"What are they pumping you full of? LSD?" I joked. I thought he was talking about Creamo, who'd just left the hospital. He'd finally decided to check out Spanish Springs mine for himself and I wasn't invited as he and some old fool he convinced to join him were planning to 'pack heat' and all I was packing was bear spray.

"No, no, no. Not the good detective. I was speaking of Professor Lopinsky. He was here earlier today, my dear, checking up on me."

The poor nurse struggled to prepare him for discharge as we spoke. Their medical center was not equipped for long-term patients, just overnighters. The room he'd spent the night in was more like an ICU with a row of hospital beds, each nestled in monitoring equipment and surrounded by stark white shower curtains. It was neither comfortable nor private. "Hold still, Captain Grayson," she pleaded, as she fought to get a flannel shirt over his shoulder cast.

The fact that I'd missed bumping into Professor Lopinsky left me both disappointed and relieved, the symptom of a disorder I hoped I'd outgrown. It's a toxic thing, this brew called attraction, especially beyond a certain age. It forces longing, the need for a fix, while your mind blindly gropes for the brakes.

"A crush?" I laughed. "You know—I'm not sixteen, and I doubt Mr. Lopinsky is either."

But the Captain wasn't fooled. "Ah, my dear, the best of us are forever sixteen." He paused to study my face. "However, I gather from your expression this day has been—"

"A blighter!"

Blighter! What the hell? That bold word slipped from my lips without my permission. Blighter was a term I never used. I associated it with pretentiousness and upper class annoyance. But, upon second thought, it was an oddly appropriate description of wilting frustration: a day during which nothing put in soil and watered had the remotest possibility of coming to life. And to top it all off, someone to whom I felt a strong attraction did not consider me a sideshow freak. Bugger! Blighter! Blast it all!

"I was hoping to track down Hyman's daughter," I whined, "before returning home with my tail between my legs. I really did like my job. The theater is a hoot."

"You're leaving?"

"Yeah, there's a four o'clock bus back to Vegas. I'm not any help here really. I contacted a few people I know in high places and told them everything. Hopefully they'll do something. But I gotta face it. I'm no detective. And as for providing any psychological help, well, I can't analyze myself out of a paper bag."

"Ahhh," he sighed in sympathy. "But I got the impression from—what was that detective's name?"

"I'm sure he's got another name, but the only one I know is Creamo."

"Creamo, yes. I got the feeling—perhaps wrongly—that all was not in vain, that you were in possession of a scintillating new clue. Something, I gather, having to do with Spanish Spring, and that's why he's driving all the way out there."

"Let me put it this way. That man has a one-track mind. If a young lady disappears, sex must be involved. It stems from . . ." I was digressing. Did I want to blame Freud again? "Never mind where it stems from. I wish it was something he could be cured of, but last time I checked, there was no cure for being a man."

"Ouch!"

"Present company excluded, of course. I hope he finds the girl out there, I really do, but I doubt it."

"You should approach every day as if it will bring you exactly what you hope for. Look at me—am I dwelling on our forced landing? Au contraire—what an excellent opportunity to prove my skills! I've never taken off from a plateau, my dear! Never! I'm filled with youthful vigor! Alive with another prospect to escape a lingering death in diapers!"

"Oh, Lord," the nurse sighed, as she slipped a pair of slippers onto his feet. "Captain Grayson, will you please stop wiggling? Your poor wife is going to have her hands full with you."

"And I'll have my hands full of her, my dear," he sighed. "As she dresses, bathes, and feeds me. Ah, yes. My hands will be all over her many . . . ahem, assets."

The very thought of his wife sent him into a litany of superlatives regarding her feminine virtues that bordered on X-rated. The nurse rolled her eyes as he spoke, looked at me, and shook her head. "I'm going to get the doctor. He's got to sign the release papers. Are you sure you feel safe alone with him?"

"Sure," I chuckled.

After she left, he tried to shift the conversation back to Professor Lopinsky. What an interesting man! Such a good sense of humor! And such a good heart! The sort of man who would be lovingly devoted!

On and on, and although I was secretly delighted, I felt like telling him he was wasting his breath. I was leaving on the four o'clock bus. That was it. Other people have romances, get married, children, the whole shebang, but not me. I lived on my own (except for my cat). I had tried to live with someone once. My husband, a giant-sized man-boy whom I mothered and, according to him, smothered. Smothered. Cripes. I bought him the car of his dreams, put him through college, and found him a job. And what was my reward? Herpes. And then after I kicked him out, I still couldn't manage to get rid of the louse. Every failed relationship of his somehow always managed to land at my front door. Women demanding to know why my ex-husband had cheated on them. By inference, they could understand why he'd cheated on me. I was intimidating. (Intimidating was another of his favorite words, channeled back at me through his numerous bimbos.) By contrast, they were accommodating, sweet natured, and most importantly, understood the sensitive, freedom-loving, happy-go-lucky (his words again) nature of the giant man-boy. Whereas, I evidently did not.

Cripes. I'd finally had to move across country. No, never again, not for me. I was leaving on the four o'clock bus.

Captain Wug's wife appeared on scene just as the nurses were considering mixing libido-killing drugs into his meds. I wish I could say she had a calming effect on him, but it was exactly the opposite. Lord have mercy, I thought, no wonder they had eight kids. They quickly determined that I must go to lunch with them. I didn't argue, of course. I was sick to death of the bland coffeeshop food.

Then I had them return me to the hotel.

CHAPTER 24

IMMIGRATION, which even the war has not stopped, will land on our shores, hundreds of thousands more per year from overcrowded Europe. I intend to point them to the gold and silver that wait for them in the West. Tell the miners from me that I shall promote their interests to the utmost of my ability; because their prosperity is the prosperity of the Nation, and we shall prove in a very few years that we are indeed the treasury of the world.

–LETTER FROM ABRAHAM LINCOLN TO GOVERNOR NYE OF NEVADA, APRIL 29, 1864

Lopinsky watched as a couple of "tall, straight, skinny gents" led a petite blonde to a double-cab truck whose bed was jam packed with electronic devices. He'd been on the hill above the old Spanish Spring Mine for almost an hour, figuring that whoever packed up the truck would soon be leaving, and then he could get shots of the old mine for his book. It was by far the biggest and most intact mine he'd encountered on Cavalry Peak.

Waiting hadn't been a hardship, he later told me. He had a pile of documents he'd charmed out of the ladies of the local historical society to keep him occupied—copies of letters from early magistrates in the area to Governor Nye, Nevada's first governor, that were most intriguing. The governor evidently found himself in a pickle. He'd been commissioned by Lincoln, largely to support the president's plan to promote western mining as a solution for postwar unemployment, something which he knew would require further sacrifice from a group of people who were already struggling against the ranchers and the railroads: the Indians. Nye knew that for Lincoln's plan to succeed there had to be peace. Peace always meant compromise. Compromise always meant loss. And it wasn't like the Indians were unaware of what headed their way. Among the papers was this warning:

They will come like the sand in a whirlwind and drive you from your homes. You will be forced among the barren rocks of the north, where your ponies will die; where you will see the women and old men starve and listen to the cries of your children for food.

–Numanga of the Pyramid branch

He glanced down at the mine. The truck had just begun heading southwest. As soon as it was out of sight, he packed up the documents, piling each neatly in the banker's box, just exactly the way he'd received them. He took the same care with his own notes, making sure each idea was duly credited. It was tedious but necessary work, a habit he'd learned over the years but which was increasingly impossible to teach his impatient students. Still he kept on trying. Annotate your research as you proceed: who, what, where, when. It will save you a lot of work in the end.

He was nearly finished when he heard the sound of an engine approaching from the north, and looked down into the ravine. A black Jeep, crept slowly towards the mines, stopping behind the crumbling mill. Two men emerged. One walked to a position in hiding at the corner of the building, while the other cautiously strode toward the trailers. The man in hiding drew a pistol and stood flattened against the wall, his head peering around the side as if preparing to provide backup should gun fire erupt. The other man stepped up to the door of the trailer, knocked, and then stepped back to a defensible position at the bottom of the stairs.

When there was no response, the driver knocked again with the same result. Then he slithered over to the second trailer. Again he struck out. He shrugged his shoulders at his partner in hiding who promptly emerged and together they picked through the area like a couple of chickens searching for feed. Finally they were bold enough to peek through the window of one of the trailers and rattle the front door. The latter action set off an ear-splitting alarm. Both men quickly spun east, west, north, south to see if the alarm had smoked out the inhabitants, but no one appeared. After a few minutes, it became apparent that no one was within earshot and so they smashed open the doors and spent several minutes rummaging through whatever had been left behind.

At that point, Lopinsky decided to leave. It was three o'clock. Soon the sun would begin to set. Not a good time to be off-roading in the desert.

He'd found me waiting in front of the hotel, bag at my feet.

"Oh, good grief," I sighed, after he told me his story.

"What?"

"That was Creamo you watched play cops and robbers. And the girl may have been Meredith Hyman."

The Greyhound bus arrived four minutes early. It pulled up in front of us, blocking the sun and causing the temperature to drop to an icy forty degrees. Lopinsky boldly scooted closer until I could feel the warmth of his body next to mine. He was dressed in a tweed jacket and thick grey cords, the type that only very thin men should wear. He was close to forty, I guessed, a youngish forty but old enough to have been married at least once. However, for reasons I can't properly articulate, I knew he was single and had always been, much to the relief of a doting mother.

The bus driver opened the door and announced a smoke break, causing a dozen or so people of all ages to emerge. Some waited for their luggage as this was their final destination; others wandered into Hotel Ely or stood on the wooden sidewalk and smoked. They had ten minutes, and then the bus would take off to points south, eventually reaching Vegas. I could be home by ten o'clock. Well, not really home, but under the bright lights of Vegas looking for a taxi.

"The young guys you saw with the girl sound like Cal and Luke," I finally said. "I did tell you about them, didn't I?"

"Oh, yeah. I kind of figured that out."

"Was there an older man, with greyish beard and glasses, with them?"

"Not that I could see—unless he was already in the truck."

"Was the girl tall and unusually pretty?"

"I was on the hill. All I could make out from that distance was that she was a blonde, and thin."

"Hmmm."

We were interrupted by the bus driver who wanted to know if I planned to get onboard.

CHAPTER 25

"I THOUGHT YOU WERE LEAVING TOWN," the sheriff grumbled. His office was full of cardboard boxes, as was the entire station. They were moving, he explained, to a more spacious headquarters. "Let me guess. This is about Leticia Honeywell again, isn't it? They dropped her off about a half hour ago. Course I recognized her right off."

"What?"

"She was one of the girls you claim disappeared from Enev, right?"

"Right."

"Well, I hadn't seen her for a few years, but it was her. You know, I was the one who had to remove her from her grandpa's place. Child neglect," he sighed. "They were quite a mess, those girls. I had to delouse my cruiser. Anyway, they said they found her out at the Spanish Spring mine, figured she belonged at Enev, and tried to return her but couldn't get past the front gate. So I called the reformatory and found out, sure enough, she'd been released. Case closed."

With that the Sheriff plopped an empty box on his chair and began shoveling everything on top of his desk into it—photos, pencils, folders, stained coffee mugs. "Sure would like to put my feet up tomorrow and watch the Packers. Yes, I would, but instead, as you can plainly see, I'll be unpacking all this shit I'm packing up today! What a waste of my time."

"You know what this means, don't you?"

"I'm sure you'll tell me, Dr. Butters," he chuckled.

"It means there are three other girls down there. You've got to arrange a search."

"No, I don't gotta do that, lady. Soon as that little lady got herself released, she hooked up with her buddies and took off for the mines to get high. They do it all the time! Why the hell do you think the BLM is shutting down all the abandoned mines? Kids! That's why! Kids, potheads and vagrants!"

"Yes but Sheriff, Peterson told me that she'd released Leticia to her grandfather, which isn't possible because you had him in jail, remember?"

"Maybe she was released before we locked him up."

The man was impossible. Arguing with him was a waste of breath. "Well, where is the girl now? Did you turn her over to social services?"

"Ha, try reaching a social worker on the weekend, lady," he laughed. "Funny, 'cause that's when we make most of our juvie arrests. Green did file a report, which they'll get it Monday morning unless it's one of their many furlough days."

"So what did you do with her?"

"Well, they said we could let her grandpa go too, so we turned her over to him."

"What do you mean—they told you to let him go? The two guys who dropped her off? I don't understand."

"The two guys who dropped her off are federal agents, lady. The same two jokers who brought her grandfather in last week and told us we had to hold him for a few days. Turns out they didn't really want him. Evidently he was taking potshots at them from the back of a goddamn horse! They just wanted him out of the way so they could go after their real target." He slammed the sides of the box shut and shouted: "Green—I need a couple more boxes in here—and some tape!"

I was dumbfounded. Cal and Luke? FBI? "Are you sure?" I asked.

"Sure 'bout what, Butters?"

"Those two jokers who dropped Leticia off."

"Yes, ma'am. We checked them out. FBI." He slapped labels on the four-foot pile of boxes, upside down, backwards. He didn't care.

"But, Sheriff, if social services removed the girl once, don't you think they'll do it again?"

"If they ever find him. My guess is he's long gone. Only reason he hung around was her, at least that's what he said after giving us the old one-fingered salute. You know, that old coot might be unsavory, but don't you think the child is better off with kin than in some foster home? I've seen what happens to kids that come out of that system. Half of them end up in prison. Besides, they'll probably put her in a group home, which I'll tell you, lady, is just one level up from prison. Might make sense to try to save the younger ones, I don't know—but the older teens, forget it."

"So you think they've left town?"

"Duh! You'll never find them. Now really, lady, I gotta be packed before the movers get here."

"Did she say anything to you?"

"Nothing that made any sense. Something about red-haired cannibals, now, I mean, really Doc."

Lopinsky, who'd been quietly standing at my side, thanked the sheriff for his time as he coaxed me from the station. Good thing. I was itching to strangle the moron.

The greyhound bus passed us on its way out of town, turning south as the driver waved good-bye. I was stuck in Ely, for another night.

My horoscope that day should have read, "As Uranus goes retrograde, be prepared for a series of near misses, elected officials who say 'duh,' and dead-end roads." Instead it said some milquetoast malarkey about needing to go inward to find the answers I was looking for. I had to stop reading the damn horoscopes. They're always wrong.

CHAPTER 26

THE COUNTY HISTORICAL SOCIETY was housed in a back room of the library, a rough-hewn stone building not unlike others in town. It contained your standard assortment of early Nevada memorabilia: miners' shovels, rock displays, bonnets, wagon wheels, pistols, and arrowheads. Documents—letters, newspaper articles, deeds, Bibles, the papers that define lifetimes—were protected from air in glass-topped tables. The ladies of the society were tickled pink to see "the Professor" again, although probably not so happy he dragged me along. They were, as one would expect, two women past menopause and proudly native to that area of the state.

I'd waited a couple of hours at the hotel for Creamo to return, nursing the blind and foolish hope he'd found the other girls. Lopinsky did not share my optimism. He'd even cautiously ventured that the sheriff's story made sense, based on what he'd heard about the old mines and their allure to the young and reckless. Hell, from the way he spoke, there was nary a fifteen-year-old left with half a brain! It irritated the hair right off the back of my neck, but having no side of my own to defend, I kept my mouth closed. Finally when he suggested a walk over to the historical society so he could return borrowed materials, I agreed. The unending click and clatter of slots, the smoke, the flash of neon lights, all had given me a sharp pain between the eyes.

I had an awkward time explaining myself to Lopinsky's fan club. They'd heard about the "demonic" activities out at the girls' reformatory. Heard and apparently, from the looks on their faces, thought I was responsible. They were surprised to hear that the daughter of a

Vegas legend had been involved but not surprised to hear about Leticia Honeywell.

"Oh, dear." The more squat of the two sighed. Her sandy-grey hair was cut bowl-like around a flat, shiny face. "Leticia Honeywell! Poor thing."

As luck would have it, both women were retired school teachers whose love of history extended to its kissing cousin, gossip. It didn't take much coaxing (in fact, none at all) to get the extended version of the Honeywell Saga. Grandpa had appeared "from out of nowhere" ten years earlier, with two tow-haired, scrawny girls, his "granddaughters," he claimed. At first he was "not too bad." He didn't offer too many details about himself, lived in a turn-of-the-century boarding house owned by a Basque widow, got a job at the hardware store stacking screws and nuts, and enrolled the girls in the elementary school. The girls were scruffy and often smelled but didn't appear to be abused in any way. The older one was morose and behind in school; the younger a bit more outgoing, even affectionate. The teachers held out some hope for her. Their cumulative files, when they did arrive from a school in Sparks, were woefully skimpy on details. Neither girl appeared to have been enrolled in any school for very long. The teachers recommended counseling, particularly for the older girl. The grandfather seemed insulted. They dropped the recommendation. After the younger one was accused of starting a lice epidemic and a hair shaving was mandated, the grandfather stopped bringing them. He left the boarding house and disappeared. A few months later, a health inspector who was checking out the store near the Steptoe exit spotted a little, blonde girl playing in the dust behind the shack. She was covered in dirt and seemed "quite wild." The grandfather emerged from the store and threatened the inspector. The sheriff was called and the girls were removed. It was assumed they were put into foster care far away from gramps and then, as so often happens to those on the fringes, they fell out of collective concern. The ladies of the historical society were "truly saddened" to hear that the oldest Honeywell girl ended up in a place like Fort Palmer (though not surprised); I didn't tell them what happened to the younger one. It seemed a kindness to spare them the gory details.

We strolled back to the hotel as the streetlights flickered on, making puny puddles of light in the dark night. I asked Lopinsky how his research was going, if he'd found what he'd been looking for, mostly to change the subject. He hemmed and hawed a bit knowing my mind was elsewhere. I thought of telling him about the call I'd made the night before, my desperate plea for someone sane, someone with power, to bring in the damn cavalry before I scurried back to Vegas with my tail between my legs. But what if nothing came of it? What if the recipient of my call for help simply couldn't be bothered? There's no way of knowing who to trust, who changes for the better and who for the worse. No one stays the same, that's for sure.

The hotel clerk hadn't seen or heard from Creamo, but she did have a message for me from Hyman. Call me, it read. Damn, I thought. Just the man I didn't want to talk to. "If he calls again, tell him I've been abducted by aliens," I instructed her.

Lopinsky followed me to my room and made himself comfortable on the double bed, propping up a pillow and kicking off his shoes.

"You expecting to stay the night?" I asked.

"Too soon?"

"Too late. I've had the romantic stuffing kicked out of me."

"Well, we'll just have to gather it all up and stuff it back in again."

"Ha, ha. Besides, I'm sore as hell. I'm just gonna take one of my lovely muscle relaxers, climb into bed—alone—and pass out."

"Then you'll be defenseless. You'll need a protector."

He cracked me up. A protector. Undeterred by my chuckles, he continued, "Besides, I give a good back rub. Swedish-style. Here. I'll show you."

"Up and at 'em, Professor! The only thing I'm cuddling up to tonight is a hot water bottle. Now, skedaddle before I drag out the bear spray!"

"OK then. Send me off into the cold with nothing but a kiss to warm me."

Brother, what baloney, I thought, as I kissed him quickly on the cheek and shoved him out the door. I didn't need a man in my life. Not again. No, never.

The phone rang moments after he left. Absentmindedly, I picked it up.

"Where's Creamo?" Hyman growled at me.

"How should I know? Probably at some bar."

One of the girls had been found, I informed him, but then, thanks to the ineptitude of the sheriff, lost again. He seemed unconcerned.

I suggested he assign someone to find Fergus Honeywell, and he replied with a "yeah, yeah." And then he asked about the limo.

"Is it gassed up and ready to go?"

"I guess so."

"Better be clean."

"Why?" I asked.

He hung up. God damn son of a bitch didn't even ask about his daughter, I swore, as I scooted under pilled sheets, my head on the pillow. God damn son of a bitch. All he cared about was his damn limo.

Creamo eventually made it back to the hotel, in the middle of the night, drunk.

"Butters? You in there?" He shouted through the door, "They tol' me you're still here. That you missed the damn bus!"

"You sound like hell, Creamo," I yelled through the door. "Go to bed."

"I had a message the boss called."

"Yeah, I talked to him."

"Jesus H. Christ. What the hell did you tell him?"

"That you were out having a gun battle with two undercover FBI agents."

"You didn't. Christ. I need a nightcap."

"You need to go to sleep."

"I could hear those damn bats screeching at each other down in the caves—what a racket. Goph said they were singing."

"Goph, I take it is the idiot who went along with you. Bats don't sing."

"Well, maybe these were a special kind of bats! Like those Rhinobackie frogs that grow babies in their mouths!"

"Go to bed."

I heard him stumbling down the hall, but not very far. Not very far at all. They'd put me in the room next to him! If it wasn't so late, I would have complained, because, on top of all his other maladies (mostly self-induced), Creamo had a bad case of sleep apnea and the rooms had walls made of paper. This meant I had to endure long periods of deathly quiet during which I was sure he'd died, followed by violent gasps as his lungs screamed for oxygen. One night it would kill him, if his liver or stomach didn't do the trick first.

Towards dawn I fell into a shut-eye state that did not require my full attention to maintain. But it was neither comforting nor relaxing. My body shut down before my brain, thus opening the floodgate to panic-driven hallucinations or the feeling that someone (the Night Hag) was sitting on my chest.

Let me sink into unconsciousness or free me, I demanded, but the Hag remained.

The technical term for this condition is "sleep paralysis," and there are many causes. Generally I advised patients who experienced this sensation to sleep on their sides, but when the Hag breathed death into my face, I am not embarrassed to admit I screamed the Lords' Prayer. I have no idea if I screamed it out loud or not, but in response I heard a male voice.

"Dr. Butters? Are you in there?"

"Satan be gone," I ordered.

"It's her." A slightly higher male voice confirmed.

"Open the door, Doc."

"Go away."

The door opened. There were steps, a click and then light filtered through my closed lids. The devil stood over me, but instead of formaldehyde and mothballs, he reeked of musky aftershave, the type young men wear.

"You called for us," he said. The voice was remotely familiar. I tried to speak, but my mouth would not obey. I tried to move, but my arms were useless. Move, body, move, I ordered. Get off my chest, Night Hag!

"She's out of it," the second man asserted. "Probably took some pills. You know how shrinks are, Cal. They take a pill to go to sleep and a pill to wake up. Then they try to tell us we're passive-aggressive. Sheesh."

"Still smarting are you, Luke? I told you—no one escapes the psych eval without some sort of label. Otherwise they'd think you were too perfect, which would be a huge red flag."

"Yeah, what label did they give you—narcissist?"

"Never mind. Toss that glass of water on her face. That should do the trick."

"You toads!" I swore. "Doesn't the FBI have anything better to do than wake folks up in the middle of the night?" I opened one eye. Then, slowly, the other. There they were. The two cowboys/caveologists/ FBI agents standing over me in khakis and striped shirts. This time they looked like models from GQ magazine.

"I thought you wanted to talk to us, lady. We got a call halfway to Salt Lake City ordering us to return immediately to Ely and talk to a Doctor Butters. Apparently that's you."

"Yes. Luckily I have friends in high places who still remember me," I explained. "Couldn't you have at least waited until a decent hour before waking me up?"

"Dr. Butters, there's a plane waiting for us in Salt Lake. So if you don't mind, let's get right to it."

"Well I'm not going to talk to you while I'm lying here naked as a jaybird. You can have a seat while I get dressed. Or you can meet me in the coffee shop."

They exchanged glances. "We'll be in the coffee shop."

At quarter to five am, the coffee shop in the Old Ely Hotel and Gambling Hall resembled, in look and feel, a model railroader's vision of early nineteen-century America, stark and artificial. Outside it was still black, and thus, the plate glass windows reflected our shallow, sleep-deprived faces like fun-house mirrors.

The young gents deflected all questions about their investigation of Gnecht, asserting only that it was a national security issue which had been dealt with.

"What was he doing down in the caves—making bombs using bat guano?" I chuckled.

"Let's just say he was accused of stealing something from the Department of Agriculture that had the department worried. We found it; end of case," Luke replied. He was thinner and younger looking than Cal, although they both looked not a day out of college. "We were told you wanted to ask about the girl we found down in the caves."

"Yes, there are three other girls down there—you need to find them too."

"We don't work on missing persons' cases," Cal explained, "unless there are special circumstances—like kidnapping, crossing state lines—that kind of thing."

"I understand, but we can't find the girl you handed over to the sheriff. She and her grandfather have disappeared. Did she say anything to you when you found her?"

"No. She was incoherent, drugged or something. She kept saying something about cannibals; red-haired cannibals. We heard her screaming—that's how we found her—in the dark, cold, and wet, as if she'd been in the river."

"Where did you find her?"

"Upstream near the . . ." Cal paused before continuing. "Near the end of the cave. We tried to return her to the reformatory, but they said . . ."

"Yes, I know. They said she'd been released."

"The sheriff said she'd probably snuck into the caves to get high with her friends. Seemed to make sense, although I don't know how they got past us. There has to be another opening that we don't know about."

"I heard the same pile of crap. But here's the thing. I think the girl you found actually disappeared the same night as Doug Hyman's daughter. You do know who Doug Hyman is?"

"Of course. With all his clout, he couldn't keep his daughter out of that place?"

"I guess it was cheaper than a golden chastity belt."

"Listen, Doc, Gnecht had the very best monitoring equipment you can buy stationed all throughout the caverns. That's how we were able to find you. If the girls had been in the caves at all, we would have known."

The waitress had finally awakened from her trance and realized she had customers. The only things available at that hour, she explained, were day-old donuts, toast, or cold cereal. The cook hadn't yet arrived.

"Separate checks," the gents ordered, after they'd requested coffee and donuts. She glared at me warily. It was too early in the morning to make things more complicated than they needed to be. Separate checks for coffee and day-old pastries? Come on, fellows.

"Expense reports," I told her, "our government in action. I'll just take toast and add mine to the tab."

I tried to get my thoughts in order, but my mind was about as useful as a corn fritter. Think, Butters, think. Outside the sky was warming.

"We can't really say anything else until we've been debriefed."

"It can't be that big a deal. I mean I just want to find the girls."

"And we have our orders."

If there's anything that'll send me to the pressure cooker fast, it's those three words: We follow orders. "I'm not going to play this game," I mumbled. "I'm going to go back upstairs and take a bath. I thought the FBI—why never mind. You're just as lazy and useless as the stupid sheriff. No, I take that back. Worse!"

After that hissy fit, I stomped upstairs. When I said earlier that my room had a bath, what I really meant was it had a bathtub: a claw-foot tub, rusty around the drain and knobs, which sat directly beneath the window facing the street. A lacy curtain fell from the ten-foot ceiling, providing a transparent canopy that almost encircled the tub. It was all very luxurious, until you realized you were on display. Every car driving past the Old Ely Hotel and Gambling Hall could see you as you bathed. I asked myself if I really gave a shit, and then decided I didn't. Took off my clothes, turned on the hot water, filled the tub, climbed in. There I percolated, head rested on a rolled-up towel until the water cooled. Still I was not willing to get out. I turned on the hot water again; this time with pink "spa" bubbles from hotel giveaways. Outside the bathroom window, the sky lightened. Winter clouds cast ominous but rootless warnings hither and thither. I heard a train in the distance reminding me someone was conscious, a cat yowl as though sadly deceived, and then hesitant rapping. I ignored it thinking, heh, old pipes.

Finally they called out. "Dr. Butters are you decent?"

"I hate that phrase! Since when is the human body indecent? Come in, boys, if you mean to be helpful. The door's unlocked."

CHAPTER 27

I KNEW LOPINSKY WAS THE MAN FOR ME when he found me chatting with two much younger men while sitting in the bathtub naked, and he skipped nary a beat. In fact, he knew who they were before the formal introductions. Maybe it was the suspicious way they questioned him upon answering my door.

"You must be the secret agents," he smiled, leaning forward to shake their hands. "I'm a Civil War historian. Max LaPlunk. Y'all are more than welcome to check me out. I think you'll find out I lead a rather boring, academic life." Thank God he had the foresight not to give them his real name.

He shuffled past Cal and Luke and took a seat by the tub in order to "enjoy the view."

"Be my guest," I chuckled. Everything risque was covered with bubbles and wash cloths anyway. I'm not that much of an exhibitionist. "The lads were just telling me about the caves."

"Are you and, ah, Dr. Butters, working together?" Cal asked as he tried to parse the relationship between me and Lopinsky. They were standing just about as far from the tub as they could.

Lopinsky winked at me.

"I told you—I work for Doug Hyman. LaPlunk here just happens to be writing a book about, well, I don't really know."

"I'm investigating a theory having to do with mining and the Civil War, which happens to be my passion. I'd like to take some photos of the Spanish Spring mine if y'all have wrapped up your operations."

"The BLM has already set up a perimeter," Cal reported. "They were just waiting for us to finish our investigation, and then they were planning to move in. Once they're finished closing down the mine, no one will be able to get down there again." He turned to his partner, "Luke, why don't you go down and check on our friend? Check the radio too—I have a hunch our orders will change again."

Luke dutifully exited stage right but not before pointing out the time. We'll miss the plane if we don't leave fast, he muttered. Cal seemed unconcerned.

"Why doesn't the state consider opening the caves up for tourism? Like the Lehman Caves," Lopinsky asked, after Luke was gone.

Cal chose his words wisely. The problem had to do with the bat colonies in the caves. They were an extinct species. That was it; end of script.

I asked him if the agriculture department cared so much about the bats, why would they sentence them to death by sealing them in? How would they get out to feed if the mine entrance was sealed?

There are other entrances, he explained, chasms in the rock bats could fly through but humans couldn't enter—like the hole they'd dragged me up after our first meeting. Gnecht's initial and legitimate task had been to determine the species of bat in the caves and figure out their survivability options if the mine was closed down. That was before he'd gone wacko.

"Did you find any hieroglyphics while you were down there?" Lopinsky asked. "Wall paintings?"

"We did—near the end of the cave. Gnecht claimed they were some kind of a warning."

"What did they look like?"

Cal thought a minute. "They were fairly simple." He took a hotel pad from the night stand, made a few quick drawings, and handed it to Lopinsky.

"Do they make any sense to you, Max?" I asked.

"Not my area of expertise, but in Major Olivore's letters, he did make reference to Osceola, a Seminole whose tribes scattered to the west after his death, often with escaping slaves. I'd like to take some rubbings of the . . ."

He was interrupted by Luke who burst into the room to report their orders had not been changed. "But, you know that big limo that was parked out in front?"

"Yeah," I replied.

"It's gone."

The water had gotten cold so I reached for a towel. As I rose from the tub, all three men turned their backs. I chuckled. "Evidently none of you has ever been backstage at a Vegas show during costume changes. Go on, Luke. What about the limo?"

"Some half-dressed dude came running out of the hotel a few minutes ago, jumped in the limo, and took off down the road."

I glanced out the window. Sure enough, the limo was gone.

"Oh, good grief," I grumbled. Hyman's phone call finally made sense. "Hand me my bra and panties, LaPlunk. We've got to get out of here."

"Huh?"

"The bra!"

"I don't understand."

"The Prince of Darkness is on his way!"

* * *

Doug Hyman didn't like what he saw below. A small asphalt strip not much wider than the highway running next to it. A smattering of small planes arranged hither and thither on the adjoining tarmac proved to him that it was sloppily managed as well.

"What on earth? We can't land on that." He scowled. He should have learned how to fly his own damn jet. Other Vegas CEOs flew their own damn Lear Jets so how hard could it be. But he'd never had the patience to go through all those hours of training required and now his fate rested on the narrow shoulders of the skinny young pilot with the sweaty palms. He thought of threatening the kid—you better not crash this beauty; she's worth more than you'll earn in a lifetime, but on second thought, that might make him nervous and prone to mistakes. Better to give him a squirt of confidence, or better yet, an incentive.

He made his way to the cockpit. "Look kid," he began, "if we survive landing on that postage stamp of a runway, I think I'll take the limo back to Vegas. I knew this place would be primitive, but look at that runway, kid! You'll be a goddamn genius if you can land on it without killing us!"

The pilot ignored him. "Please return to your seat, and fasten your seatbelt."

Hyman refused. He reminded the imp just exactly who owned the plane.

"Alright," said the pilot, "stand there. But if the runway is full of ruts, which looks to be the case, no pile of money will be able to stop you from hurling through the windshield."

"Christ," Hyman snorted as he returned to his seat and did as instructed. "Remind me why we're doing this." He asked the man sitting next to him, an older fellow, white haired, semiretired—the way Hyman liked his consultants. Lure them out of retirement for a big wad of cash, and then send them back to the golf course when you don't need them anymore, that was his policy. Thus, they weren't beholden to him for a huge salary and benefits, and they were beyond the age when they needed affirmation or slapping down. He didn't understand those idiot CEOs whose entourage always contained legions of cash-strapped, ambitious young sharks. Get the old duffers out of retirement. Cheaper, less messy and no competition for the ladies.

"Because you're a good and loving father," the consultant replied.

His particular talent was public relations. The Attorney General of the State of Nevada had ordered an investigation of the notorious girls' reformatory at Fort Palmer. This in and of itself was not alarming for it was widely acknowledged, even by judges, that Enev was a cruel place to send juvenile offenders. Girls shipped to Enev for their crimes were never seen again. Never got to go to a prom, get a job at the Dairy Queen, sleep in on Saturdays. Among the many rumors, first and foremost was that it sat on the edge of the nuclear testing grounds. Six months there and your skin would be covered in lesions, your eyeballs the color of limes, warts on arms, hands, and feet, doomed to spend the rest of your life hiding in your parents' basement. Year after year the rumors persisted, but nothing was done. Now, all of sudden, an investigation had been ordered. And why? Because the daughter of Doug Hyman, de facto ruler of Las Vegas, had disappeared. By evening, it would be on the front page of the Las Vegas Sun.

The man sitting next to Doug Hyman was there to make sure that when the story ran, it wouldn't report that Doug Hyman was sitting in his penthouse office issuing a "no comment." No, it would have a picture of him at the gates of Enev, demanding to know what happened to his daughter. Cynical readers would jump to the conclusion that Hyman was planning to run for office on the family values platform, a strategy used by so many Nevada politicians so ineptly that it was a joke. But they would be wrong. Doug Hyman would never run for office. He left that to the chumps. The idiots who were willing to turn their lives inside out just so some street could be named after them. No, he was there for an entirely different reason. Vegas was about to evolve from "Sin City" to "Disneyland with Slot Machines" and he intended to be the top mouse, just as he'd been Chief Rat through the turbulence of the sixties and seventies. At first he'd thought it was a stupid idea, a betrayal of the men who'd made her. Pirate ships and roller coasters? Hotels that looked like pyramids and decadent European cities? It was a disgrace. But after he'd seen the numbers and realized the potential for added revenue with a more family friendly message, he jumped in full throttle. His resorts would transform into playgrounds for those of all ages, where the children could play and the adults could gamble.

"I do care about Meredith, you know. This isn't just a PR stunt. I do have feelings."

The PR man shot Hyman a weary look.

"I do have feelings. Yeah. I'm feeling damn lucky I only had one goddamn daughter! At least when she was locked up, I knew where she was all the time. Now she's probably with some moron getting pregnant. Pregnant. Shit, that would mean another child. I'll be a goddamn grandpa. Can you imagine? I'll be forced to accept some idiot, half-moron son-in-law shaking me down for money all the time. We need it for the kid, Grandpa Hyman—for a high chair, for a bicycle, for Yale! Hell, they'll probably name my grandson some hippie-dippy name like Phineas or Godfrey," he paused.

Did the PR man buy his story? Probably not. Doug Hyman knew he was a good liar but a piss-poor actor, which he'd told that goon from the government. But had the G-man listened? No. This is what you tell everyone, everyone, he'd said.

Fuck this shit Hyman thought as the plane touched down much smoother than he expected. Showtime!

* * *

Celebrities don't visit downtown Ely every day, so when the block-long limo that had been a curiosity in front of the hotel for three days suddenly sprang to life, burning rubber as it skidded out of town, folks started wondering what was up. This event was followed by the squeal of a Lear Jet flying dangerously low over the west end of town. The Colonel provided scant details to the curious; only that a man with an entourage had landed at the airstrip and was heading toward town.

By the time Lopinsky and I got down to the lobby, it was full of townsfolk. Evidently, they decided whoever was coming to town would be staying at the Old Ely Hotel and Gambling Hall where movie stars had stayed many years earlier when westerns were in vogue. Some were dressed as though on their way to church, with kiddies in tow. Others looked like tourists, toting heavy camera equipment. I felt like telling them they were going to be disappointed. Outside of Vegas not too many people would recognize Doug Hyman or even care who he was.

"Are you sure he wants to talk to you?" Lopinsky asked as we made our way through the crowd.

"I'm not taking the chance. Besides, didn't you want to see those cave paintings before the BLM closes down the mine?"

CHAPTER 28

CAPTAIN WUG THOUGHT IT WAS ODD to hear a knock upon his door. Casa Agila was so difficult to reach that during the winter months he and his wife retreated to a condo near their daughter in San Diego. Even in the good weather, they were forced to buy a post-office box in town, as their home was too far off the beaten path for the postman. Thus, they rarely had uninvited visitors.

"Who can that be?" his wife asked, looking out from the bedroom where she had been busy packing since daybreak. Upon seeing her glowing face, he fell in love with her all over again. She never aged, that woman, he sighed to himself. Shining always with joy no matter what. It amazed him; simply amazed him. He couldn't stop telling people what an incredibly lucky, undeserving son of a bitch he was.

But on that day, she'd put her foot down. After retrieving his precious plane (by some means involving a helicopter, the details of which she really did not want to know), they were leaving. They were flying via commercial airline to San Diego, so that he could fully recuperate from his injuries, and being that she asked for so little and put up with so much, he was forced to acquiesce. Of course, first she had to allow him to rescue his plane. It had cost them a pretty penny. But he'd been warned he was not to lift a finger to help. He was only to direct the activities of the "squadron" who'd volunteered to help: the Colonel, Captain Hank, and a team of National Guardsmen who specialized in retrieving downed aircraft.

"Perhaps the Professor has forgotten something, my dear," Captain Wug theorized as he walked towards the front door. "We did make sure they took along a snakebite kit, didn't we, my love?"

"Of course. They seemed very well equipped and so cute together, don't you think?"

"Aye, my love."

The captain's house sat on a hill overlooking the Ghost Train route and, although it was stucco and not adobe, followed the style of an old hacienda, with an atrium in the center and no front or backyard. The concrete floor kept the house cool during the summer, and a deck on the flat roof provided a place where they could sip martinis as they watched the Ghost Train chug through their private kingdom.

"Who goes there?" the captain asked through the thick barn door. "Friend, foe or ungrateful child?"

"The police," was the response.

His heart stopped. Had there been an accident—something so awful it compelled the police to actually drive out to Casa Agila and not merely call? Someone in the family? A close friend? He opened the door cautiously.

It was not the police but the sheriff. "Howdy, Captain Grayson. Enjoying your Sunday?" he asked with a note of familiarity that the older man found off-putting.

"I was."

"Sure wish I was enjoying mine, but I got a horde of reporters down at my office that you wouldn't believe . . . Say, you wouldn't happen to know the score?"

"The score?"

"He means the football score, dear," the captain's wife interrupted. She'd abandoned her packing and now stood directly behind him.

"Howdy, Mrs. Grayson," the sheriff drawled.

"We don't have a TV, Sheriff, so sadly we can't help you with any of the football scores. How about some coffee?" she asked, reassured by his friendly demeanor that no harm had befallen a loved one.

"No thanks on the java, Ma'am," he drawled. "This is a just a quick visit. You see, we found a floater this morning, out at Cave Lake. It could be that woman who went missing from Fort Palmer several weeks back, but we won't know for a while. Decomp, I hear, was pretty bad."

"Oh, no!" she gasped. "Her family will be devastated."

"You know them, ma'am?"

"Not really. We treated the mother for shock shortly after she went missing from that awful place. I think the family's from Yerington,"

"I do think you're right. What a good memory you have."

"Everything about my wife is perfection. Her heart, like Einstein's mind, should be preserved and studied. But what does this unhappy conclusion to a local conundrum have to do with us?"

"I hear that you had an accident out on Spaceman a few days ago, Captain."

"Yes," the older man admitted, "but I . . ."

"Mind telling me what you were doing out there? Even SAR avoids that area like the plague. Just taking a little joyride, were you? Ha, ha."

A joyride! Captain Wug fumed inwardly. No matter how many times he'd been told, the sheriff ignored the fact that he and his comrades worked for the US Geological Service and were not merely flying around the skies reliving their glory days. Evidently, to the sheriff, anyone over the age of sixty was a useless annoyance, prime fodder for the dog-food factory.

"I had a client who wanted to fly over that terrain."

When pushed by bad manners or bad taste, Captain Wug's voice lowered to a guttural, almost canine warning not to push any further.

The sheriff thought for a minute. "I see. I suppose the client was interested in all the paranormal activity out in those parts."

"You could put it that way."

The sheriff duly wrote down what was said and then went on to another question: "Did you see anything at Cave Lake?"

"We weren't anywhere near what you mistakenly call a lake, so sadly I cannot aid in your investigation."

"I see. And where's this client of yours now? Perhaps she or he saw something."

"I cannot confirm my client's whereabouts at the moment," Captain Wug asserted with the greatest of confidence.

("Now," Captain Wug told me later, "I thought it mighty curious that the sheriff didn't know you were my client—half the town knew."

"I'm sure he did," I assured him. "He just hadn't figured out how he was going to cover his own ass once the shit hit the fan.")

The sheriff sighed, "No big deal. I just didn't want to leave any stone uncovered, no matter how far-fetched. That's the kind of guy I am. Detail oriented," he chuckled. "To tell you the truth, I just had to get away from that goddamn office! Everything's still in boxes, and we've got all these goddamn reporters and cameramen mulling about, all wanting to know about that Hyman girl. Crap. And then the man himself comes roaring into town causing quite a ruckus. Doug Hyman, King of Vegas. Sheesh. You know . . . I bet that Butters woman is behind this goddamn investigation! You know, she and the attorney general grew up together."

The captain and his bride shrugged their shoulders. They had no idea what he was talking about.

"You did hear about the investigation, didn't you?"

Captain Wug replied that he paid very little attention to the news or politics and so the sheriff filled him in on the details, glossing over the fact that he himself was perilously close to being implicated (particularly if certain details which had not yet come forward, did come forward). "I don't know what they're doing in my office! But they're all over the place asking questions. I mean, Fort Palmer is a goddamn state facility and we keep our noses out of their business. That dumb broad is probably up for election. Goddamn mistake to put a woman in as top cop, if you want my opinion. No offense Mrs. G."

Mrs. G. nodded that she took no offense, so the sheriff continued on, "Say, Captain, what are you going to do about that old plane you ditched—junk it for the insurance?"

"Junk it for the insurance!" Captain Wug huffed. "That's a Polikarpov biplane! A little touchup and she should be ready for flight for decades to come."

The sheriff chuckled derisively, "Should I activate the air-raid sirens?"

It was a poorly kept secret that he told anyone who would listen about the old flyboys. They were a joke. A danger to society. Any day now one of them was going to have a heart attack and crash into the school; then there'd be a stink! But for now his hands were tied. If he tried to stop them, he'd piss off the anti-regulation, gun-loving shit-kickers. No elected official in the state could afford to do that!

Captain Wug had a comeback, but his wife read his mind and poked him in the back—her way of saying it makes no sense to piss off a feeble-minded man with a badge—and she was right. She was always right. That woman was perfection itself.

The sheriff closed his pad with a stiff click. "There's one more thing. We can't seem to locate Winnie Peterson. The staff at Fort Palmer says they haven't seen her for about three days, so I sent a man out to their ranch, and both of them were gone: Winnie and her husband, who's been a cripple for I don't know how long."

"I've never met the woman so I don't know . . ."

"Yeah, but her husband was a pilot during the war, wasn't he? Some kind of big-shot hero."

"Ward Peterson? No, he was navy commandant. I didn't know the man personally but, of course, I've heard of him."

"We saw him at the clinic about a year ago," his wife interrupted. "He was in pretty bad shape, failing kidney, blood pressure through the roof. And suddenly he recovered; in fact he even began wiggling his toes. We have no idea why."

"When exactly was that, Mrs. Grayson?" the sheriff asked.

"I'm afraid I can't tell you for certain. You'll have to check with the hospital."

"I understand. My momma can't remember where she puts her glasses sometimes and has to call me up to come find 'em for her! Gets real excited 'cause she's missing her favorite soap. Ah, the joys of getting old, hey?"

I can only imagine the venomous gaze the sheriff received for that zinger. He apparently left soon after, wishing the two a pleasant afternoon while bemoaning the fact that his was going to be a nightmare, a fate both the captain and his bride later told me was too good for him.

CHAPTER 29

THE SPANISH SPRING MINE had a large entrance that forked about fifty feet in. One fork led several hundred feet into the side of the mountain and then ended. Evidently this had been the more productive tunnel, happily mined for at least a couple of years before they'd decided to drill in the opposite direction. There were numerous side shoots, dug into the mountain to follow a productive lode. Men's names and the dates they worked the mine (or died) were carved into the petrified beams. A rusty rail line running down the middle indicated that the mine had enjoyed a large margin of success at one time.

"What were they mining for? Gold?" I asked Lopinsky. He'd been gentlemanly enough to carry all the equipment in his backpack—dozens of flares, first aid kit, canteens, and energy bars, stuff that Cal and Luke had given us before they took off.

"Silver ore," he replied. "Acanthite or galena. No doubt they were looking for gold, but in this area they found mostly silver ore, until of course, they stumbled onto copper, but that was in the early twentieth century. You know, there's a common misperception that the money from the mines in Nevada was used for the war effort, and that's why it was admitted to the Union. But the real story is far more complicated."

By now I'd ceased to ask "what war." There was only one war in Lopinsky's mind. The Civil War. On our long drive to Spanish Spring he told me just about every oddball story, myth, legend, controversy, statistic, campaign, battle, and type of armament having to do with the war. Any subject I introduced led gradually and seemingly back to an interesting antidote about "the war." With any other person, this tendency would have been annoying, but it was part of Lopinsky's charm. Even the announcement over the radio that the attorney general's office had just launched an investigation into irregularities at the Eastern Nevada Girls Training Facility, inspired another Civil War anecdote:

"Did you know that the man uniformly considered the worst Union general once ran a school for juvenile delinquents?"

"No, I can honestly say that I did not."

I was thinking about Ruby O'Tannen, the young girl I'd taken under my wing so many years before. Look at who she was now: The Attorney General! The Top Cop. And I had been a part of her metamorphosis, helping her through those troubled-teen years to an ebullient, brilliant future. Not only had she remembered me, but, she'd immediately ordered an investigation based on my word alone! Of course, it was a crock of bull, which I like to think I would have seen through were not my head so far up another part of my anatomy. Luckily I kept my raving ego to myself, as Lopinsky continued his tale.

"His name was Benjamin Franklin Butler, but in the south he's known simply by the title: the Beast of New Orleans."

"The Beast of New Orleans? Heavens! What did he do? Steal their fine china?"

"Oh, no. Something much, much worse. Something unspeakable to a Southerner. This outrageous horse's ass besmirched and impugned the reputations of the fine white women of New Orleans!" he laughed. "Yeah, he tossed them into the pokey for daring to look askance at horny Union soldiers. And guess what he charged them with?"

"Spitting on a vile Yank?"

"Nope. Applying the tricks of the world's oldest profession. Ah, yes, these fine Southern belles, with their lace petticoats, dainty umbrellas, and frail dispositions were tossed into the slammer with white-trash women, pickpockets, and whores and forced to toilet with the coloreds! Oh, the indignity of it all. Fine Southern women thrown in jail and branded as whores for what? Rightfully spitting in the faces of presumptive Union scoundrels who were worse, in their minds, than the most uppity of coloreds."

It was too easy to laugh with Lopinsky. Much too easy.

"But they got back at him," he continued, both hands on the wheel as a strong wind threatened to knock us into the sagebrush. "Damn. Is it always so windy out here?"

"This? This is nothing. Don't you get hurricanes where you're from?"

"Chapel Hill's a bit inland. Most of the south is soft, hot, moist, and gooey. Till of course a twister comes along. Anyway, back to my story. I have in my possession—I'll have you know—a genuine chamber pot with the Beast's arrogant puss painted on the bottom, circa 1864. It's one of my proudest possessions. I'll let you use it, if you're nice to me."

"Oh, no, not really? A chamber pot? Isn't that where . . ."

"Yes, ma'am. I understand they were quite the rage in the South's finer homes, where they referred to their pissing pots as butlers, in honor of General Butler, of course."

The Civil War, he explained, had always been his passion, even though his great grandparents (both sets) had immigrated after The War, settling, not in the South but in North Dakota. He theorized that his obsession was not really with The War but with a culture that could capitalize on such a dark event, churning out endless novels and movies, enactments of battles that perpetuated myths and glorified the deaths of child soldiers. No other country had romanticized an internal conflict to the point of comical stereotypes that were so entrenched in its culture.

Lopinsky was the youngest of three boys and, he had to admit, the smartest. He had excelled in debate, while the other two studied math, without much ambition but out of a duty to practical immigrant parents. Thus he was expected to be the flake: an actor or a showman, a loser. Accordingly, it had been quite a surprise to his family when his obsession with debate and history landed him a scholarship to Columbia while his sibling's sturdier math skills only netted them passage to state colleges. After Columbia, he'd headed south, spending years teaching history in small Southern towns just to "get a feeling" for the area before he went back to school for advanced degrees. He never returned to North Dakota.

The second tunnel was much more primitive than the first, the ground uneven, the framing blackened as though there had been a fire. There were no signs of serious chiseling into the side of the mountain, no names carved into the beams. As we crept down the tunnel it seemed to shrink, the ceiling growing lower, and the walls closing in.

"Either I'm growing or this tunnel's shrinking," I chortled. "One pill makes you taller, the other makes you small. Where's the White Rabbit?"

This led to, yes, another Civil War anecdote: "You know General Lee set up one of his headquarters in a cave. Yup. In Missouri. It's not nearly as beautiful as some of the other caves in the South, but it is big. One of the "rooms" as they called the caverns, was large enough to fit eleven hundred Confederate—eleven hundred Confederates—now that's some . . ." he stopped midsentence.

A soft, cool breeze licked my cheeks and the tip of my nose, causing the hair on the back of my neck to tingle. He felt it as well.

"Hey, I think we're getting close—smells like, what is that smell?"

He put down the lantern and pulled a massive flashlight from his backpack, shining it ahead into the dark.

"Holy Crapola!" I gasped.

"Wow!" uttered Lopinsky. Beyond a jagged fissure in the tunnel wall we could see massive fang-like stalactites.

We'd found the caves.

CHAPTER 30

AS TO WHAT HAPPENED NEXT, I didn't put all the pieces together for a long, long time. One minute I was in a cave examining hieroglyphs, and the next, in Chapel Hill six months later, living a more-or-less peaceful life with the poor gent who'd gotten stuck with me. At first I remembered only the explosion, the dust, and then waking up under a quilt in Nebraska with the equally confused Professor Lopinsky. Evidently he'd flown us from Ely to a cornfield airstrip in Nebraska in a trance, under what opiate I know not. The farmer, whose house we both woke up in, was little help. His main concern was that we leave, at daybreak, with nary more than a corn muffin.

"What's going on? I feel like I'm in a goddamn Hitchcock movie," I'd asked Lo as he started up the Cessna.

"I don't know, but Farmer John is anxious for us to leave, so I say, let's get out of here and figure it all out later."

"Where are we headed?"

"According to the flight plan he gave me, Chapel Hill."

"Your home."

"Yes. It appears that someone wants us there."

It was a drippy and cheerless day in the Midwest. For most of the flight, we stayed under the clouds, dodging lightning as brutal weather pummeled the heartland. We didn't say more than a half-dozen words. I kept thinking that the next morning, things would all make sense. But then, things got even stranger. Beginning with a phone call from Lopinsky's publisher.

"Ecstatic" and "over the top," were words he showered on Lopinsky with regard to his first drafts, offering a prodigious advance for the final, but only if it were completed by a certain date. Lo, who'd been suffering under the strains of the "publish or perish" mandate that claims so many talented professors, quickly jumped at the bait. Then came the call from Captain Wug, wanting to know if we'd arrived safely and filling us in on the news. Meredith Hyman and her friends had been found. When I heard where and how, I knew I couldn't return to Nevada and remain sane. And so I volunteered to stay and help Lopinsky with his book, an offer which, given the short deadline, he was more than happy to accept. I have to admit it was a hoot, deciding which of his many pictures to include, annotating every frigging quote, revising, revising and then revising again. We worked side by side at his dining room table, as slowly my memory began to return, clunks flooding by like marshmallows in a muddy stream. If Lopinsky remembered anything past the explosion, he never admitted it. His focus was entirely on the book: from morning to night, the book. The house went to pot, we ate only takeout, our hair grew long and we freaked at any unnecessary break in completing "the book." However, sadly, Lo's final draft failed to ignite the fickle fancy of the publishing world. Therefore, when his sabbatical ended, back to classes he went. As for me, well, enough time had passed that I could have returned to Vegas and resumed my old life, but I liked having my feet massaged every night by a man who was still a boy. A boy, only in that wonder-filled way we all should be. And, though it pains me to admit as much, I had been infected with the I-can-write-a-best-seller, lethal, deadly, and often contagious virus.

"Should I begin with the ending and tell it all as a flashback?" I asked Lo.

"What's wrong with just simply telling it?" He was running late, shuffling through papers to find one that had gone missing. We were in the bookshelf-crammed "parlor" of his midcentury bungalow, a modest brick house in Chapel Hill. The decor was surprisingly modern for a historian: low, flat couches; redwood-burl coffee tables; and a number of "blankies" strewn about for reading sci-fi on a cold night.

"Because when I tell a story, I ramble. I begin in the middle and expand all around the subject until I can make some sense. Most of the time at least. Don't laugh! The telling is so much easier than the writing!"

"Write it as fiction."

"I guarantee it's going to sound like fiction. Come on Prof, you're the writer—where do I start?" I pleaded, wondering for the umpteenth time if he was jealous that I'd intrigued a publisher with my inquiry and deciding that he was not. The one thing I'd learned about Louie Lopinsky in the six months we'd been together was that he never gave up trying. If he couldn't sell an idea to one publisher, he'd find either another idea or another publisher. In the case of Lincoln's Role in the Snake Wars, Lopinsky's publisher claimed his manuscript was "too scholarly." I suppose they were looking for something more along the lines of Lincoln's Gay Cabana Boy. At any rate, unfazed, he moved on.

His experience in publishing had led me to deep misgivings: worries about what some neophyte editor would do to my manuscript, should I ever write it. They'd probably insist that one of my not-so-fictional characters undergo a complete transformation. Transformations were key, I'd read in one of Lopinsky's many books on how to write a best seller. At least one of your major characters must undergo a radical transformation or your book will sell as fast as garlic ice cream. Oh, I suppose I could force a transformation. But whom should I force to have a life-transforming experience? Creamo? Hyman? Me?

"You're forgetting about 'Manifestations of Pubescent Telepathy'." Lopinksy reminded me. "You wrote that."

"That was a serious case study that was exploited into a made-for-TV horror docudrama by some slimy bastard–Hollywood asshole! It was because of him I left psychology."

"You could have sued. You know I'll keep your toes warm no matter what you decide to do, but right now I've got to go. There's a group of freshmen, mighty fine Sons of the South, dying to tell me how misinformed I am about the Civil War and its causes."

"My goodness. You'd better go straighten them out. I'll just suffer alone."

I couldn't imagine Lopinsky as anything but a professor. He relished fulfilling every stereotype of the profession, except the red bow tie: wearing the corduroy jacket with the patched elbows, smoking an occasional pipe with chums in the local coffee shop, having students over for wine and cheese, walking across the campus as the leaves changed color and fell, smelling of freshly opened books and chalk on the board. It was more than his life; he'd grown into his dream. I was the envious one, trying on so many professions, none of them fitting comfortably. Would I ever figure out what I wanted to be when I grew up? It certainly seemed doubtful.

After he left I sat in front of the typewriter like a dummy. There was still so much I didn't remember, and some memories—well, who knew if they were merely figments of my imagination. The blank, white page was more like a black hole.

I looked out the window for salvation and found only further temptation to goof off. Spring had walloped the southeast with an LSD-inspired brush, igniting the wisteria growing untended over Lopinsky's iron fence into a veritable firestorm of magenta. Lo wasn't much of a gardener, relying on the services of a Mr. Chang, who came by once a month to mow the small patches of grass in the front and rear yards when the weather was nice. All necessary trimming and weeding had been ignored, and thus the backyard was a jungle of native species run amok. Now they were roaring their magnificent roars.

Alas, like the garden, I was untrimmed. Unfocused. Generally when feeling coltish, I meandered to the campus to breathe in all those monumental thoughts of the young, but on that day I craved solitude. So I opted to walk over to Battle Park, a primitive forest smack-dab in the middle of town. There, amongst the trail options was The Vale of Ione, a path in the "easy-to-moderate" category alive with finches rustling through the poplars and chipmunks chasing each other in circles chattering, creatures unencumbered by the things in life we humans feel are requirements for happiness, a sense of purpose, and worth. And a goal, ah, yes, a goal. And a plan. Where would we be without plans?

I realized as I puttered along that meandering trail that a reordering of my own requirements was definitely long overdue. What were my "musts" in this life? Simple. I must eat, sleep and play with the cat.

Nice to do (but not necessary) would be: driving seniors to their medical appointments, learning origami or taking a watercolor class.

However, last on the list was writing a book. What requirement did it satisfy? Purpose and worth. Two things that drive us all into knots. For crying out loud. A life doesn't have to have a purpose any more than a bird has to have a reason to fly. And worth? A situational equation based on other people's needs and wants. I didn't have to write the true story about Fort Palmer. What would happen if I didn't? There would still be forests, free to walk through. Birds to watch soar through the sky. No, I could return the advance and tell the publisher to forget it. Maybe the university could use another lecturer on Jungian dream theory or the local theatre a prop person with experience in a real-life Vegas theatre. Yes, there were endless possibilities in this world—no need to do something that caused as much discomfort as writing a goddamned book.

I spotted a young coed sunning herself on a flat rock next to a creek and thought instantly of Meredith Hyman, the sweet, confused daughter of the King of Mean, now far away from Pastel City in the green hills of Switzerland. What lucky girls were Bonny and Thanh to be included on that particular magic-carpet ride. Too bad all of the girls hadn't been saved. The coed waved her hand over a nearby patch of spring anemones as though stroking them. They fluttered at her touch. The web of magic closed around me as I stood spellbound, my mind blissfully empty of thought.

The sensation was broken by far-off sirens. Somewhere there was pain; somewhere there was always pain still, that one moment of zen had rebooted my overwrought brain. I skipped back down the hill, sniffing every budding rose, sticking my tongue out at toddlers in nanny-powered baby carriages, and barking at dogs who barked at me. The old Fi had returned.

When I got home, there was a young man standing on the doorstep in grey, pressed slacks and button-down shirt—trim, straight, and oh-so-serious. He gave a little wave as I approached.

"Do you remember me?" he asked.

"Of course. If I remember right you're a cowboy. No, you're a caveologist. No, you're a secret-agent man. What are you really, Cal?"

"A Scorpio."

The quip took me by surprise. "Touché. How did you find me? The Bureau?" I asked, leading him toward the kitchen at the back of the house.

"Hell no, Spanish Spring was a ghost operation."

"Ghost operation?"

"Yeah. The only person who has all the pieces of the puzzle is a ghost. Someone you've never heard of and you can't track. You get your orders, you don't ask questions, and then you disappear."

"Ah . . . Say, would you like an iced tea?"

He nodded and then took a seat near the window as I pulled two cans of Nestea from the fridge.

"Then how did you find me? Captain Grayson?"

"Yup." He popped the tab off his drink and took a sip. Then he put the can down on the small round table we used for coffee in the mornings, making sure to set it on our one and only coaster—a freebie from a local brewery.

"Ah." I sat down across from him. He wasn't half–bad looking: earnest grey eyes, clean shaven, well groomed, but so guarded. A missing mother, I thought. Or perhaps he was gay and afraid to come out. That was one of the things I missed the most about Vegas. The openness. The willingness to be whatever you are. That certainly wasn't the case in Chapel Hill. "Is the Captain still in San Diego? Lo and I haven't talked to him in, I dunno, a couple of months at least."

"Yup, but his wife says he's itching to get up in the air again."

"I can imagine. But what led you to him?"

"Luke. He told me that when he dropped you two off at the airstrip, he ran into an old timer who recognized you and demanded to know what was going on. God knows what Luke said to him. I didn't ask."

"Aha. That makes sense. But why go to the trouble of tracking me down? Not that it isn't a hoot to see you again and all but . . ."

"I . . . I . . ."

I chuckled. "I hope you don't think I know any more than you do, 'cause sad to say, I didn't remember anything about that day until weeks later, and even now there are gaps in my memory that refuse to close. But when Captain Wug described the man who'd dropped us off at the airstrip, I knew it had to be Luke, which meant you couldn't have been too far away."

"You're wrong. I didn't arrive at the airstrip until later and by then Luke was long gone." He paused. "Dr. Butters, for six months I thought we'd killed you and the professor."

"Killed us?"

"I was there when they dynamited the entrance to the mine. In fact, it ate at me so much that I quit the service as soon as I got back from Thailand. I didn't join up to kill innocent civilians."

"How noble of you, but as you can see I'm doing just fine and dandy. Oh, I miss my job 'with the circus' as Lo puts it. May I'll even go back someday when he comes to his senses and realizes what a bad deal he got," I chortled. Cal did not. "So you got shipped off to Thailand, but what about Luke?"

"He's in DC. A desk job. I bumped into him last week and told him I was resigning and why. He told me I was being silly because you weren't dead."

"They split you two up? What a shame. My favorite pair of G-men! What is the world coming to?"

He chuckled. "Luke got demoted. Even though he doesn't see it that way. My guess is he pissed off the agent in charge by asking a few too many questions, and everyone knows you don't ask questions on a ghost operation."

"Yes, indeed! Can't have any of those pesky questions. Listen, he didn't happen to say where he picked us up from, did he?"

"Peterson ranch."

"How interesting. I wonder how we got to Peterson ranch from . . . Oh I know. Never mind. That part I do remember."

"You've lost me."

"Say, how did we get all the way to Nebraska? They didn't let Lopinsky fly . . ."

"Someone flew you there."

"Aha, the plot thickens." My cat finally figured out I had company. Meow, she howled at the back door. "I hope you're not allergic to cats, because I'm afraid she'll yowl until we let her in, the little minx! She still misses Vegas." I got up to let her in. "She's gotta be where the action is."

"Doc, you probably won't believe me, but we were halfway to Salt Lake with Gnecht when we got the call that our orders had been changed. Five minutes later, the heli swooped down out of the sky, and the next thing I knew, Luke and I are back at Spanish Spring watching fellow agents set explosives at the opening even though they were fully aware civilians were inside. After that I was just following orders.

'Find an ex-cop named Banhof and follow him,' I was told. 'After he takes the bait, let us know.' Then off they flew. I was about to leave when your friend Captain Grayson and his pals arrived in a massive Chinook to see what was going on. They said they were retrieving a plane he crash-landed, supposedly on Space Man plateau, and heard the explosions."

"Yup, his pride and joy. A WWII biplane. I'm surprised he didn't tell you the whole story."

"He was worried about you and the Professor. But then he saw that your car wasn't there and . . ."

"Where was our car?"

"Luke drove it over to the ranch."

"Oh yeah. I should have figured that one out. Duh. So you followed Creamo."

"Creamo?"

"The ex-cop. On foot?"

"Oh, they also had a Harley on the Sikorsky."

"The Sikorsky."

"The helicopter."

"Oh, good grief! What a fandango! Listen, you want a brownie 'cause I think I need one. Unfortunately, they're cannabis free. I think pot makes brownies too dry, don't you?"

I retrieved the Panda cookie jar from the counter and set it in front of him. He had a peculiar expression on his face as if he had no idea what on earth I was talking about. "It's only ten o'clock in the morning," he said.

"It's always time for a brownie!"

Sheepishly he searched for the tiniest one he could find. Then he nibbled on it slowly. I've never understood people who nibble on food, art, or life. "Good boy. Have another bigger one. You're such a skinny guy. By the way, whatever happened to your friend, Dr. Gnecht? Did they just leave him by the side of the road to rot? That would serve him right after what he did to me. The bastard!"

Cal chuckled. "Sorry to disappoint you but we handed him off to another agent and gave him the honor of driving that lunatic to Salt Lake City. I figure the only reason that they went out of their way to pick us up is 'cause we knew the terrain and they wanted to get in and out fast. They didn't want to risk having an agent get lost in the desert."

I sat down across from him and helped myself to a brownie, remembering what a blast Lopinsky and I had the night before smoking a bit of pot and attempting to cook. Ha. We're both such batter-aholics that it was a miracle any of the batter made it into the oven. "What a hoot!" I croaked. "Whoever directed the Spanish Spring gig should really start running Vegas extravaganzas and give up undercover secret-agent stuff! He'd make more money than working for the government, and I can assure you, it would probably be a lot more fun, but then I imagine the element of danger is probably what most agents crave and not plain old ordinary fun."

"You're the shrink."

"By the way, what was the bait?"

"It looked like a fax but I have no idea what was on it. I found the ex-cop in the hotel lobby pacing the floor in front of the clerk."

"With a drink in his hand, no doubt."

"Right. When it finally arrived, he tore off north toward the ranch."

"It was probably a search warrant."

"But he's no longer a cop."

"It's Nevada."

"Oh."

"Did you get to witness his dramatic rescue of the girls? I swear, ever since I read the news articles I've had such a hoot envisioning good ole Creamo sneaking up on Peterson ranch, gun in hand, poking through the old buildings until finally hearing the girls' cries. What a happy fellow he must have been thinking he'd solved the case! And the girls. What must they have been thinking? If they were thinking anything at all. They'd probably been tranquilized too. So tell me, is that how it went down?"

"Probably" he chuckled. "But I didn't get to see it. After Bahnhof (or Creamo or whatever you want to call him) took off, I radioed the agent in charge and then got my next set of orders, which were to wait in a car parked behind the hospital for the 'packages.' Sure enough, about an hour later, three girls came out the back door dressed as nurses. I knew right away they weren't nurses—they were too young. And then it dawned on me that they were the three girls who'd disappeared from the reformatory and that somehow the whole operation might center on them."

"Did they say anything?"

"Nah, and I didn't ask any questions."

"Oh yeah. I remember that 'no questions' thing."

"Anyway I drove them to the airstrip as ordered, bundled them onto a Lear Jet, and watched it take off. Then I took off for Reno. I had a ten o'clock flight to catch."

"That would have been Hyman's Lear Jet. The slimy toad flew up to Ely just so he could be on hand for his daughter's rescue and pose for some pictures. You know, I knew he was involved somehow. Probably not from the beginning but definitely at the end. There's no way he would offer to pay for the girls' tuition at a fancy boarding school out of the kindness of his heart. Give me a break! He has no heart. I nearly lost my cookies reading the garbage they printed in the papers."

Cal took a final sip of his Nestea. "So that whole story about the polygamous cult was . . ."

"Unadulterated hokum. Fodder for the masses longing for torrid tales of sexual debauchery. They did an audit of the release records at the reformatory and found a few discrepancies, not as many as I'm sure Creamo expected but enough to shut it down finally. Don't get me wrong. It deserved to be shut down but not because Winnie Peterson was selling girls to sex traffickers or polygamous cults!"

"These brownies are good, but you were just kidding about the cannabis, right?" he asked, taking another brownie.

"Was I?"

He smiled. "You were. I can read the body language, you know. Say, did that ex-cop ever figure out he was part of a sham?"

"I doubt it. He's in some small Mexican village, living off the huge reward he got from Hyman for saving his daughter!"

"How about the Peterson's? Did they ever find them?"

"That's a joke! 'They' are not even looking for them. I bet they're living on an island somewhere courtesy of Uncle Sam. God knows they can never go back to Nevada. The press would have a field day."

My old grey cat decided to hop on Cal's lap for a pet. Generally she scratched any poor slob who attempted such a maneuver without proper foreplay, but she was in a forgiving mood that morning. Undoubtedly a half-eaten bird carcass (which I would some day find lying under one of the lilac bushes) was the reason.

"Dr. Butters, where were the girls if they weren't at Peterson Ranch?"

I knew the minute I saw Cal standing on my doorstep that he would ask that question. I just didn't know how to respond.

"I believe that the girls, like Major Olivore before them, stumbled onto a place the government is now trying to keep secret, which I'm happy about because God knows what would happen if people knew it existed. However, I'm far too cynical to believe their motives are entirely altruistic. Imagine a tribe of Indians living in a crevice in the earth, not quite the width of a football field and the length of two city blocks, with pueblo-like enclaves carved into the cliffs—reminiscent of the Anasazi. But despite the lack of direct sunlight, there's plenty of vegetation. Each cave dwelling appeared to have its own garden, with vines growing down from the ledges. Fascinating really. Too bad the professor was in a trance. He would have loved it. The rumble of the water was deafening. I guess that's why the Major called it Echoing Waters. Anyway, these residents are quite unusual. They're empaths."

"Empaths?"

"They don't speak. They communicate via ESP. If I had to guess, which I'm piss-poor at doing by the way, I'd say they developed that trait over centuries living in a crevice where the sound makes it impossible to communicate. But it could have been all the nuclear testing done just west of them, who knows. I'm sure some branch of the intelligence community is trying to figure it out as we speak."

"Where is this place? We were all over that area."

"I'm not sure. I remember the explosion and then—wham, bam, thank you ma'am! All hell broke loose. Bats clogged the air, screeching in panic, zillions of them! I can assure you, that's not something I ever want to experience again. Hysterical bats! Someone grabbed us and began dragging us down a long narrow passageway but I couldn't really see anything because of the dust and the bats! Next thing I remember was a canoe ride down an underground river, like those you see in the Yucatan. I put out my fingers to touch the rocks to make sure I wasn't dreaming. It was so damn beautiful, Cal, like some kind of a friggin' fairy tale. Poor Lo was on another planet. I tried talking to him but nothing. 'Come out of it, dammit,' I said, shaking him. Then I heard a voice in my head saying very clearly 'he is in the shadow world' and realized someone was reading my thoughts. But instead of getting paranoid because someone was in my brain, I felt relaxed. Strange, huh? That's why I think they're empaths and not just telepathic."

Cal didn't look up or comment. He just kept stroking the cat as she purred. I took a sip of iced tea and continued with my story.

"A man was waiting for us when we emerged, standing on the beach near to that damn whirlybird, wearing dark aviator glasses with a baseball cap pulled down low. You know, I can't remember the faces of the Indians who rescued us no matter how I try. I guess it was the shock, or maybe they can erase certain memories, I don't know. But I do remember the man's face, well, what I could see of it through the dark glasses and baseball cap. He looked just like Sidney Poitier, and I just love Sidney Poitier, don't you?"

"I didn't catch the similarity."

"Really? Oh yeah, he was a dead ringer. I saw him once, the real Sidney Poitier that is, in Vegas. He was with his wife, a blond lady who was quite pretty, as you can imagine. I think they were there for a boxing match. That had to be, oh, I dunno, four years ago. Say I bet you've seen a lot of famous people."

"Not really."

"Hmm." I began to see why Cal was single. Having a conversation with him was like cleaning the fridge. "Guess I mentally waddled away from my story, didn't I? I always do that. Used to drive ole Creamo crazy, but Lo's the same way so we get along. Huh, between the two of us, well, sometimes it'll take three days to get to the point."

Again no response, so I continued. "Truth to be told, there's not much else to tell. I was dying to snoop around because I've always been fascinated by empaths but we were hustled into that giant hunk of metal and wham, bam, thank you, ma'am, we were in the air! That bird sure is fast—it must have cost Uncle Sam a pretty penny. I looked down and the ground had completely swallowed the crevice. It was probably an optical illusion caused by the desert sun, but maybe it was a cloaking device. You know, like on Star Trek. You do watch Star Trek, don't you?"

"I don't think we've developed cloaking devices yet, Doc."

"It was a joke! Anyway, that's all she wrote. Can't remember the rest."

Cal continued stroking the cat. As he did, she shed voluminously. Huge fuzz balls that fell to the floor and would probably find their way under the table, the stove, and even into the garden like tumbleweeds. I was surprised that he listened without scoffing. Lopinsky, well, he had his doubts when my memory chunks surfaced. Underground rivers, mind-reading Indians. All things I could have dreamt, he claimed, but I knew I had not. I blamed that publisher's call, coming so soon after we arrived in Chapel Hill that it couldn't have been a coincidence. It played the role of diverting all his attention to his book and away from anything that might have just happened to us. Amazing how proximity to a dream can be so intoxicating. "So what are you thinking?" I finally asked Cal. He was being too quiet.

"I think I might have seen them, the Indians, I mean. Every now and then I'd see something in the shadows or hear a voice that sounded human when there was no one around. But why do you think they brought back one girl and left her where we could find her and not the others?"

"Oh, Leticia. Lordie, Peterson had her on so many meds that reading her mind was probably like skipping through a land mine. On top of that, she had a wacko grandfather filling her head with stories about red-haired cannibals."

"We had a few run-ins with the grandfather," Cal sighed, shaking his head. "Apparently he thought we were in league with the cannibals and tried to scare us off by taking potshots at us from the back of a horse," he paused, looked me in the eye, and grinned. "That was one hell of an assignment."

"It's . . ." I prompted.

"I know what you're going to say, Doc. It's Nevada."

"That's right. So now what will you do?"

"Hmm." Cal gently put Felicity on the kitchen floor and rose from his seat. It was time to go, he explained. Time to retrieve his resignation before it got into the wrong hands. I told him I thought it was an excellent idea and walked him toward the front door.

"You know what's funny?" he said with a twinkle in his voice. "This whole thing happened because of a century-old journal."

THE END

MORE GREAT READS FROM BOOKTROPE

Don Juan in Hankey, PA **by Gale Martin** (Contemporary Comic Fantasy) A fabulous mix of seduction, ghosts, humor, music and madness, as a rust-belt opera company stages Mozart's masterpiece. You needn't be an opera lover to enjoy this insightful and hilarious book.

Forecast **by Elise Stephens** (Young Adult, Fantasy) When teenager Calvin finds a portal that will grant him the power of prophecy, he must battle the legacies of the past and the shadows of the future to protect what is most important: his family.

Holding True **by Emily Dietrich** (Contemporary Fiction) Born in the hopeful energy of the civil rights movement, Martie struggles to live out the values she inherited by founding the Copper Hill commune, with tragic results.

A State of Jane **by Meredith Schorr** (Contemporary Women's Fiction) Jane is ready to have it all: great friends, partner at her father's law firm and a happily-ever-after love. But her life plan veers off track when every guy she dates flakes out on her. As other aspects of Jane's life begin to spiral out of control, Jane will discover that having it all isn't all that easy.

Jailbird **by Heather Huffman** (Romantic Suspense) A woman running from the law makes a new life. Sometimes love, friendship, and family bloom against all odds... especially if you make a tasty dandelion jam.

Discover more books and learn about our new approach to publishing at **booktrope.com.**

Made in the USA
San Bernardino, CA
07 September 2013